STARSTRUCK

In the wings

STARSTRUCK

In the wings

DIANE REDMOND

Hodder
Children's
Books

a division of Hodder Headline plc

CONTENTS

For Isabella – of course!

CHAPTER ONE

★

The New Girl

If it hadn't been for Mr Forest's new job Belle would never have made the great move from north to south. She'd never have met her best-ever friend, Yasmin Khan, and never have discovered the Cambridge Children's Drama Club. But these were in the future. Events which would unfold and change her life. Right now Belle was furious.

'You're only taking the job for the money,' she fumed when Mr Forest announced the forthcoming move.

'Of course I'm doing it for the money, Belle,' her dad had answered patiently. 'With a growing family to keep I can't afford to ignore a substantial pay rise, especially when my youngest daughter has ambitions to be an actress,' he'd added with a warm smile.

Belle hadn't smiled back but behind her grumpiness she knew her dad had no choice. Her brother, Chris, was at university in Bristol, her sister, Claire, was doing GCSEs, she was at primary school and her little brother, Ben, was still at playgroup. Even with Mr Forest working all the overtime going and Mrs Forest working part-time they were still pushed to pay the mortgage every month. When a new firm on the Cambridge Science Park phoned up and offered Mr Forest a job, plus car, it really was an offer he simply couldn't refuse.

Belle had hated saying goodbye to all her friends and relatives but when it came to saying goodbye to her class teacher she'd broken down and cried. Sarah Hughes had been the best thing in her life. She had spotted from the start that Belle had a talent for acting and had encouraged her to join the after-school drama club, instilling in her a deep love of the stage. Sarah was sad to lose Belle but over and above her own feelings was a real determination that Belle should continue with her acting.

'There are bound to be excellent facilities in Cambridge,' she'd said at their final tearful meeting. 'You must promise me that you'll go along.' She waited for Belle's sobs to subside. 'Promise,' she urged.

'I . . . I will,' Belle had answered sadly. 'But they won't be as good as your classes,' she'd said, tears filling her eyes all over again.

'They'll be much, much better,' Sarah assured her. But her predictions didn't turn out to be quite true, as Belle was to discover when she started her new school on a golden bright morning at the end of October.

Belle felt awkward in her new uniform with its stiff white shirt and itchy, red pleated skirt. Her shock of long, straight, white-blonde hair was held back in a velvet band but she knew it wouldn't stay there for long. It was quite unlike other girls' hair which always seemed to stay in one place. Hers had a will of its own and whenever she got excited it framed her face like a dishevelled halo. Belle's big brother always teased her, saying she looked as if she had electric currents running through her which made her hair stick out! In contrast to the wildness of her hair Belle had the loveliest, dreamiest eyes. Large, sky-blue, fringed with long dark lashes and emphasised by beautifully shaped black eyebrows. Her nose was small, upturned and flecked with soft golden freckles, and her mouth was wide and constantly on the edge of an irrepressible smile. As Belle scrutinised her uniform in the full-length bathroom mirror she scowled.

'My feet look enormous in these new black shoes,' she cried.

'Your feet are enormous,' her older sister mumbled as she brushed her teeth in the basin.

'I know that,' Belle grumbled. 'But these shoes do nothing for them.'

When she and her mum arrived at the Charles Darwin Primary School Belle was completely fazed by the size of the impressive red-brick building near the city centre. It was much bigger than any school she'd ever attended before, with huge playing fields all around. Just before nine o'clock Belle and her mother went to see the headmaster, who welcomed them warmly, then she was on her own! As she sat at her desk Belle sneaked a quick glance at the other students who all looked far too posh and smart for her. Suddenly her eyes lit on a lively-looking girl on the other side of the classroom. She was tall and willowy slim, with a soft brown complexion, huge eyes the colour of golden honey, and the longest, raven-black hair Belle had ever seen. The girl smiled warmly at Belle who instantly beamed back. In the playground they made a beeline for each other.

'Hi, I'm Yasmin Khan. Jazz for short.'

'I'm Isabella Forest. Belle for short. Hi!'

Laughing, the new friends wandered across the

teeming, noisy playground chatting about everything – school, the other kids, their favourite subjects, their worst subjects, and finally their hobbies.

'Drama,' they both said together then gazed at each other in complete delight.

'I don't believe it,' Jazz gasped, her eyes as big and bright as stars.

Belle couldn't believe it either. 'Excellent,' she said. 'Do you have a school drama club?'

Excitement faded from Jazz's face as quickly as a light going off. 'Drama club – here?' she scoffed. 'No chance.'

'Why?' Belle asked. 'We had one at my other school. It was brilliant.'

'I'm sure it was,' Jazz replied. 'But you'd never get any of these teachers starting one up. Chess, computers, football, cricket, pottery, French, swimming,' she said, going through the long list of after-school clubs. 'But drama, no way.'

'Couldn't we suggest one?' Belle asked.

'I tried that but nobody listened. They might if some parents backed us up, but a drama club is the last thing my mum and dad would like to see me at,' she finished gloomily.

'Why?' Belle asked.

'They don't *approve*,' Jazz explained, snootily emphasising the last word.

'What's wrong with a drama club?'

'First of all they think it's frivolous nonsense and second, they'd go bonkers if I told them I wanted to be an actress.' Seeing Belle's baffled expression Jazz went into a little more detail. 'We're Bengali. I was born and brought up here like all my brothers and sisters. We have different attitudes to our parents who aren't as strict as some Bengali parents I know, but they're still strict enough. The theatre's not the sort of place they'd want their daughter to work in. At a push they could just about be persuaded that set design or costume was OK, but singing, dancing and acting – forget it!'

Belle smiled at Jazz's vividly dramatic way of telling a story. It was a pleasure just listening to her.

'What about your parents?' Jazz asked. 'Do they approve of acting?'

'They don't mind,' Belle answered. 'As long as it doesn't interfere with my work. They want me to do ten GCSEs, like my sister, Claire, and go to university, like my big brother, Chris.' Belle pulled down the corners of her mouth. 'They just don't understand how serious I am about acting.'

'How did you get into it?' Jazz asked.

'I've loved it for as long as I can remember,' Belle said, her blue eyes blazing with passion. 'I used to drive my family crazy, dressing up all day long and running about the house pretending to be a witch or a fairy queen.'

'Me too,' Jazz said. 'I remember forcing my family to sit on the sofa while I sang Bengali songs until they were blue in the face. The best thing of all was getting to wear my mum's fabulous silk saris and her jingling silver jewellery. She used to go mad at me for nicking her stuff but I tell you, it was worth the ticking off just to feel that good.'

It was soon time to go back into class but they continued their talk during the long lunch-break and discovered that they lived only a few streets away from each other.

'I'll take you to Midsummer Common on our way home,' Jazz said. 'It's only round the corner.'

Belle had arranged to meet her mum at the school gates at three-thirty.

'Mum!' she cried, wide-eyed with excitement. 'Can I go to Midsummer Common with my friend? It's only round the corner,' she added, repeating Jazz's words. 'I won't be long.'

Mrs Forest nodded. 'Be careful and be back by five, before it gets dark.'

Midsummer Common was an enormous green lined with big, old chestnut trees loaded down with conkers. There was a children's playground with a paddling pool on one side and a bigger, more adventurous playground for older children at the other.

'Wicked!' Belle cried as she and Jazz tore across the park and jumped on to the swings.

With the autumn wind whipping across their faces, sending their hair flying out behind them the girls laughed as they swung higher and higher into a blue sky dotted with scudding white clouds.

'You know,' said Jazz, as they slowed down a bit to catch their breath, 'there's a drama club in town. I've seen it advertised in the library, but I've never dared go along on my own.'

Belle slammed her feet on the ground so hard she nearly did a triple somersault!

'You *what?*' she demanded.

'A drama club,' Jazz repeated. 'At the library, in town.'

'Let's go,' Belle said, grabbing Jazz's arm and hauling her off the swing.

'I can't,' Jazz said. 'If I'm not home by five my mum

goes crackers.' Seeing the look of disappointment on Belle's face she quickly added, 'But we could go after school tomorrow.'

'Brilliant!' Belle enthused.

'Cool it,' Jazz warned. 'I'm sure the club's really popular. It's run by Helen Powers – ouch!' She yelped as Belle squeezed her arm.

'Helen Powers! The actress in EastEnders?'

Jazz nodded.

'Yes. Now let go of my arm before it drops off!' she laughed.

'I'm sorry,' Belle said, quickly releasing her arm. 'I'd no idea Helen Powers lived in Cambridge. Imagine *her* teaching at the local drama club – wowee!'

'Yeah, wowee,' Jazz echoed flatly. 'Everybody will have the same reaction as you and there'll be a waiting-list from here to eternity.'

'Maybe Helen Powers will spot our amazing talent the moment we walk through the door and offer us a place – just like that,' Belle said with a loud click of her fingers.

'I'm sure she will,' Jazz answered, joining in the fantasy. 'I mean, who could resist a dynamically dramatic duo like you and me?'

CHAPTER TWO

★

The Dynamic Duo!

As soon as school finished the following day Jazz and Belle ran across Midsummer Common and arrived at the library hot and over-excited. They found the drama club poster pinned up in the entrance lobby, between ones for a self-defence course for women and Yoga classes for the elderly.

'Here!' Belle cried as her eyes lit on the poster. ''Helen Powers' Children's Drama Club for eight to twelve year olds,' she said, reading out loud. 'Every Saturday, two till five. The Library Theatre, fourth floor. Excellent!'

'Look at this,' sighed Jazz, handing Belle a glossy pamphlet. 'The Cambridge Children's Drama Club's Christmas production. *The Wizard of Oz*. Wouldn't you die to be in that?'

'Yes,' Belle answered absently. 'But right now I'm much more interested in contacting Helen Powers. Can you see a phone number anywhere on the poster?'

Both girls had their heads pressed so close to the

poster that they didn't notice somebody walking up behind them.

'Can I help?' said a clear, familiar voice. They turned to look into the smiling face of Helen Powers, the famous actress.

'Are you interested in the drama club?' she asked. Gob-smacked, the girls nodded.

'You might have to go on the waiting list,' Helen warned. 'We're a bit over-subscribed at the moment.'

Disappointment snapped Belle into action. 'How long is the list?' she asked politely.

'Pretty long,' Helen answered. 'I only wish I could do two classes a week but it's the time, you know.' Seeing disappointment written huge across the girls' faces Helen added kindly, 'I'll tell you what. Why don't you come along to the drama club this Saturday just to check it out. You never know, you might hate it.'

The girls beamed from ear to ear. There wasn't a moment's doubt in their minds that they'd love it.

'Yes, please!' they answered simultaneously.

'OK, see you Saturday then,' Helen said. 'Must dash. I only popped in here to pick up some theatre tickets. Bye.'

The girls cycled home across the common with its horse chestnut trees blazing gold against the slow-setting sun.

'That was a real stroke of luck bumping into her,' Belle raved, thrilled to bits that she'd met Helen Powers face to face.

'But she did say they were full up,' Jazz reminded her. Belle just smiled and winked.

'You never know,' she teased. 'Something might turn up.' How could either of them have ever guessed exactly what!

Belle counted down the hours to Saturday but by Friday Jazz had a face as long as a fiddle.

'What's the matter with you?' Belle asked, astonished. 'Tomorrow's the big day. Buck up!'

Jazz shook her head, on the verge of tears. 'My mum says I've got to stay in tomorrow afternoon.'

'What?' Belle spluttered. 'You can't possibly stay in.'

'That's exactly what I told my mum; not that I mentioned the reason why,' Jazz quickly added. 'That would have really freaked her out.'

'So what did you say?'

'That I was meeting a friend at the library.'

'And she won't let you go?' Jazz shook her head glumly.

'My Aunt Nandita's coming with her new baby and I've got to help mum make tea and gurgle sweet nothings in the baby's ear.'

'You can't!' Belle cried. 'You just can't!'

'I know,' Jazz assured her. 'But tell me how I'm going to dodge my mum's clutches.'

'Tell her I'm the new girl at school. Really s-a-d!' Belle emphasised the word so much Jazz started to giggle. 'No friends, a bit thick,' Belle added, really getting into the part. 'Tell her you feel sorry for me and you're the only person in the whole school who likes me.'

Jazz laughed. 'I don't think I'll go quite *that* far,' she said. 'My mum would finish up feeling really sorry for you and invite you for tea too!'

'Say whatever you think's best,' Belle said. 'Just be there tomorrow – or die!'

*　　　*　　　*

At one-thirty the next day Belle walked into the library, early for probably the first time in her life. She'd been up at a ridiculous hour, worrying about what to wear. By ten o'clock she'd tried on every article of clothing in her wardrobe and rejected them all. They were either too fussy, too babyish, too small or too tatty. She wanted to look cool and trendy, not like a little girl going to her first party. In despair she dashed into her older sister's attic bedroom and said, 'Have you any clothes I could borrow?'

Claire, still half asleep under the duvet, waved in the direction of her wardrobe and turned over. Nearly everything was miles too big but in a plastic bag at the bottom of the wardrobe Belle found a pair of mulberry-coloured velvet leggings which she measured against her waist and legs. Tucked into her boots nobody would see they were too long and they'd go brilliantly with her black tee shirt and jade green velvet waistcoat.

'Thanks, Claire,' she called as she ran out of the room.

The next problem was her hair. Should she leave it wild and loose or try and keep it back in a velvet band? Deciding that velvet was the theme of the day, Belle grabbed a brush and scraped her hair back into a high, swishing ponytail.

Pleased with the finished effect, Belle ran downstairs for a very late breakfast, then jumped on her bike and set off for town. When she got to the library she nervously climbed the many stairs to the fourth floor, following the signs for the Library Theatre. Once there Belle hung back, rather overawed by the elegant glass-fronted foyer. A man held the door open for her and gulping hard she thanked him and hurried in. Comfortable black and grey chairs and sofas were ranged around glass-topped tables in the reception area, and from the coffee bar drifted the most delicious smell of freshly ground coffee and hot doughnuts. Belle sat self-consciously on a plush sofa close to the door, flicking through a Library Theatre programme as she curiously watched different groups of people coming and going. She beamed with relief when Jazz came dashing in.

'Hi!' Belle called. Jazz saw her but instead of joining her she ducked into a shadowy corner where she pressed her back flat against the wall. Belle walked over to her and smiled.

'Jazz, I know this is the drama club but aren't you going a bit over the top?'

'Shh!' Jazz hissed as a tall, handsome, Bengali boy walked in. The boy instantly spotted Jazz.

'Yasmin! Come home immediately,' he commanded.

'No way,' Jazz replied, tears swelling her enormous topaz-yellow eyes. 'I'm staying *right* here.'

Seeing how upset she was the boy softened his tone and said quietly, 'Jazz . . . what're you doing?'

'I'm meeting my friend,' said Jazz, nodding Belle into the conversation. 'And then we're going to the Children's Drama Club.'

'Drama club!' the boy cried, his anger rushing back. 'You're mad!'

'Jamal,' Jazz said, 'we're going along to watch. The club's full up, with an enormous waiting-list. What's the problem? I've not exactly got the main part in *Cats*, have I?' Jamal didn't look convinced by her argument.

'Why do you keep lying to Mum?' he asked. 'One of these days, Jazz, your lies are going to land you in a lot of trouble, you know.'

'If I told them the truth I'd be in a whole lot *more* trouble,' Jazz replied angrily. 'And nobody will know anything – not unless *you* split on me.'

The boy shrugged and started to walk away.

'Jamal, you won't split, will you?' she begged.

'So what do you want me to tell them?' he demanded. 'A pack of lies, like you?'

'Anything, just cover for me, *please*,' she called after him. Belle could see that even though the boy was angry he couldn't say no.

'Oh, all right!' he snapped, and turning on his heel he walked out. When he'd gone Jazz slumped on to the nearest sofa.

'That was my charming brother, Jamal,' she said.

Belle didn't have a chance to ask one of the many questions burning on her lips. Luke Whelan, a boy in the year above them at school, walked into the foyer and headed straight for them.

'What's he doing here?' Belle wondered.

'Hi. Looking for the drama club?' Luke asked.

The girls nodded self-consciously.

'Come on then, follow me,' he replied.

'Do you go to the drama club?' Jazz gasped.

'Sure I do,' the boy answered casually. 'I've been coming here since I was eight.'

Swinging open heavy, double doors he led them into an enormous hall with a stage draped in heavy red velvet curtains.

'Big, eh?' he said, catching the girls' stunned expressions. 'You should see it when all the seating's out. It holds about four hundred, you know.'

Luke showed them where to hang up their coats, then joined a group of older children, all cracking jokes and laughing loudly. Belle and Jazz stood awkwardly at the side, wishing they looked as cool and trendy as the rest of the kids coming in. They were relieved to see Helen Powers, who welcomed them with a warm smile and asked their names.

'Good to see you,' she said. 'Here are some application forms for you to fill in.'

Belle and Jazz tried to fill in the forms but their attention was constantly dragged back to the kids wandering into the hall.

'I've counted sixteen so far,' Jazz whispered.

'They all look so much older than us,' Belle said.

'There are two girls over there who look about our age,' Jazz pointed out.

Two jolly-looking, tall girls, clearly twins, giggled and smiled at them, and a pretty, graceful girl with wonderful long golden-auburn hair and huge silver-grey eyes smiled too. A rather noisy, glitzy-looking girl with short, cropped blonde hair and narrow, slanting cat-eyes simply scowled. Luke joined Belle and Jazz and explained who the people were.

'Daisy Belham-Thomas is the pretty one,' he said. 'The cheerful twins are Rozzie and Millie, don't ask me who's who, I never can tell, and the girl giving you the evil eye is Tracie Long. Don't take it too personally,' he joked. 'It's her way of being friendly.'

'Who's he?' asked Jazz, nodding towards a large black boy prowling around the back of the hall. He wore a Yankees baseball hat backwards and had a ring in his nose.

'Jerome,' Luke replied. 'He's cool. Know what I mean?' The girls nodded but they weren't actually at all that sure they knew what Luke meant.

'OK, before we start,' Helen called over the chatter, 'let me introduce Jazz and Belle who are here to check us out.'

The group, obviously used to being observed, just nodded and smiled. Jazz and Belle tried to look confident as they smiled back, but both of them were shaking in their shoes!

'To work,' said Helen.

In a circle they did some warming-up exercises, breathing deep and shaking out their arms and legs, then Helen dropped down on all fours and began to paw the ground and growl.

'Simple Simon says . . . roar like a wounded tiger.' As she spoke Helen padded in between the kids, sniffing their clothes and their hair. Laughing they copied her movements. Some paced the floor, limping and whimpering; others stopped to sniff or stretch or yawn. One boy grabbed another and turned him over to gnaw his leg.

'They're good,' Belle whispered to Jazz, who nodded in agreement but didn't for a minute take her eyes off the action.

'OK, Jerome,' said Helen. 'Your turn now, but stick to animals. Simple Simon says what?'

In one quick movement Jerome was on his feet and beating his chest. 'Make like an old gorilla!' he said with a wicked smile that completely transformed his former hard-man expression.

The pretty girl, Daisy, hunkered down on the floor, scratching her armpits. Luke ran round the room, slamming his chest with his fists and grunting, while the twins, Rozzie and Millie, giggled so much they could hardly do anything at all. In the half-hour that followed the group laughed themselves silly as they frisked like gazelles, leaped like panthers and cackled like hyenas.

'Excellent,' called Helen, clapping her hands together. 'Take five.'

As the children sprawled out on the hall floor, gasping for breath, Helen walked between them dropping costumes at spaced intervals, then put a collection of props on the stage. A telephone, a silver hairbrush, an egg-timer, a mirror, a fan, a hairdryer, a broom, a feather-duster, an old-fashioned musical box and a teddy bear.

'OK, this is what you have to do,' she said. 'Work with a partner and devise a three-minute improvisation based on the costume and the prop you've chosen. Only one prop per couple,' she added. 'You have ten minutes to devise a sketch, then we'll see what you've come up with.' As the group split into couples Helen turned to Jazz and Belle and said, 'Do you want to give it a whirl?'

Without a moment's hesitation they were on their feet, dashing across the hall for the nearest costumes. Jazz grabbed a crinoline-style wedding dress and Belle found an old black leotard, full of holes. By the time they got to the stage there was only one prop left, the musical box.

'Now what?' puzzled Jazz, staring at their weird collection. Belle stared too, then got suddenly very excited.

'If I keep my T–shirt on under the leotard I could mime being a strong man in a circus,' she said, struggling into the dusty garment.

'Great idea,' said Jazz, stepping into the faded

wedding dress. 'We could do an old-fashioned circus act.'

Jazz wound up the musical box and to the tinkling music Belle flexed her muscles and started to wobble and strain as she pretended to lift heavy weights. As the music faded away Jazz picked up the box, rewound it, and mimed a quaint Victorian waltz. With her raven-black hair hanging loose about her face, which was set in a demure smile, Jazz played the part perfectly. All too soon Helen shouted over the noise and laughter, 'Time's up. On with the show.'

Luke and Jerome went first and had the class in stitches as they pretended to be two drunken men having an argument. Luke, who was a natural-born mimic, cowered and trembled as Jerome towered over him, threatening to punch him. Belle and Jazz were enjoying themselves so much they forgot about their turn until Helen called out their names.

'Come on, we've got to get used to the limelight,' urged Jazz. Their little sketch seemed to take hours to act out but when it was over Belle checked her watch and was astonished to discover it had only taken two minutes from start to finish.

'That was fun,' said Jazz, as they sat down to loud applause.

'Great,' Belle agreed. 'The longest two minutes of my life!'

The last hour of the afternoon session was the rehearsal slot for *The Wizard of Oz*. Seeing the girls' wistful faces Helen suggested they stayed to watch. Both nodded eagerly. The very last thing they felt like doing was leaving the drama club and going home. As Helen ran lightly up the steps on to the stage a big, middle-aged lady with an extremely loud voice came swanning across the hall in pink dance shoes, yellow leggings and a bright pink tee shirt.

'Hello, darlings!' she cooed as she sat down at the piano and began to play the opening chords of 'Follow the Yellow Brick Road'.

'Elvira will take this lot through their opening song and dance routine,' Helen said, pointing to the line of Munchkins on stage. 'I'll be working on Dorothy's scene with Scarecrow and Lion.'

Elvira had a wonderful voice, loud and powerful like an Italian opera singer. She and the Munchkins burst out singing, '"Follow the yellow brick road, follow the yellow brick road. Follow, follow, follow, follow, follow the yellow brick road."'

'What wouldn't you give to be up there doing it with

them?' Belle whispered as she desperately tried to restrain herself from joining in the singing.

'Anything,' Jazz answered dreamily. 'They could do with a few more too,' she added as she counted down the line of Munchkins. 'There are only eight of them.'

'Thinking of volunteering?' Belle teased.

'I wouldn't need asking twice,' Jazz replied. '*And* I've had singing and dancing lessons too.'

At the other end of the hall Helen was working with Daisy, Luke, Jerome and a big boy she called Karl. Daisy was Dorothy, Luke was the Scarecrow, Karl was the Tin Man and Jerome was the Lion. Tracie Long, the scowling, bad-tempered girl, had the most appropriate part – she was the Wicked Witch of the East! When she whooshed in on her broomstick Jazz and Belle giggled so much they nearly fell off their chairs!

Towards the end of the session Helen brought the main actors on to the stage where Daisy sang 'Somewhere over the Rainbow' accompanied by Elvira. The girl not only had looks, style and grace, she could sing like a bird.

'She's amazing,' gasped Belle as the song finished. 'Why do some people get born with everything?' she added enviously.

'Are you talking about me again?' Jazz teased.

Suddenly it was five o'clock and the session was over.

'Well done, everybody,' Helen called.

But nobody was in a hurry to go, they all just stood around laughing and chatting. 'Come on, I know I'm irresistible,' said Helen, clapping her hands together. 'But please, drag yourselves away. I've a senior class queuing up outside. Go home! See you all next week.'

Belle noticed that Daisy Belham-Thomas didn't hang around with the rest of the group. She nervously skipped down the steps and hurried across the hall for her bag and coat. An elegant woman, with the same wonderful hair and eyes as Daisy, was waiting for her, nervously rattling her car keys. She smiled briefly at the girl then they both dashed out of the hall.

As Belle was saying goodbye to Helen she suddenly had a brainwave.

'I know you're full up,' she said. 'But you really are a bit short of Munchkins, aren't you?' she finished in a blurt before her nerve gave out.

Jazz stared at her in total disbelief but Helen looked thoughtful.

'I am actually,' she answered. 'The main cast is so large it's left me short on the chorus line.'

'If you need any extras, we've both had dancing and

31

and singing lessons,' Belle said, praying that Jazz wouldn't mind her speaking on her behalf.

'I'll think about it,' Helen answered, smiling, as she slipped their forms into her bag. 'Have you put your telephone numbers on these?' Both girls nodded. 'Good,' she said. 'Thanks for coming. We'll be in touch.'

'Be in touch!' Belle cried once they were out of the theatre and in the foyer. 'How many times have I heard that line in films. I wonder if she *really* means it?'

'It's like being given a peek of heaven then asked to leave,' sighed Jazz. 'Still, that was a stroke of genius, Belle, saying there weren't enough Munchkins in the chorus line.'

'Bit of a cheek, really,' Belle admitted. 'I hope you didn't mind me saying you'd had singing and dancing lessons?'

'Of course not,' Jazz replied. 'Anyway, I have had singing and dancing lessons. Bengali singing and dancing lessons to be precise!' she added with a laugh.

'Come on, let's see if we've got enough money for a Coke,' Belle said, emptying everything out of her pockets.

Between them they found just enough for a Coke, with ice and lemon, and a Kit-Kat too. Sitting in the foyer cafe the girls savoured every mouthful. It was only then that Belle remembered Jamal.

'Does your brother always follow you around?' she asked.

'Only if he smells a rat,' Jazz answered. 'He heard me telling mum I was meeting you but he knew I was up to something – he always knows when I'm up to something. So he followed me.'

'Will he tell your parents?' Belle asked.

'No,' Jazz answered confidently. 'He's not a sneak and he's never mean. He just worries about me. It's really difficult for him being the eldest son and feeling *responsible*.' Jazz sighed. 'He feels both Bengali and English, I just feel English which makes my life a lot simpler.'

Suddenly she spotted the time on the foyer clock and jumped sky high. 'I've got to go,' she said, grabbing her coat and rucksack. 'If I'm not home by five-thirty I'll be in deep trouble. Bye, Belle. See you on Monday.'

Belle cycled home slowly, deep in thought. Up until now she'd always thought her parents were a drag when it came to her passion for acting but when she compared herself to Jazz she realised just how lucky she really was. As a new, silver-bright moon appeared in the pale evening sky Belle smiled and thanked her lucky stars.

CHAPTER THREE

★

Under Pressure

Unfortunately Belle was a bit hasty in thinking herself lucky. Parental pressure was on as parents' evening loomed large in two weeks' time.

'I'm dreading it,' Belle moaned to Jazz over their tuna pasta lunch. 'The school are bound to push computers and my dad'll go for it and insist I join the wretched after-school computer club. Yuck!' she said, shoving her plate away.

'Is that yuck to the pasta or computers?' Jazz giggled.

'Both!' Belle answered.

'My parents will be awful too,' Jazz commiserated. 'They had nothing but glowing reports from this school when Jamal was here. I'm the bad news. Could do better, should try harder, lacks motivation. That's what I get on my reports. Why can't they think *creative*,' she sighed. 'That's where they'd find the real me. Instead they keep trying to recreate another scientific genius, like Jamal.'

The banana custard pudding was even worse

than the first course. 'Let's get out of here before I'm sick!' muttered Jazz.

In the school playground the girls moodily walked up and down, munching on an old apple Belle had found in her rucksack.

'Wouldn't you die for a place in the drama club,' Jazz sighed dreamily. 'Imagine going along there every week and being one of the crowd.'

'I'd settle for a Munchkin!' Belle answered, dead serious.

Quick as a flash Jazz said, 'Is that an alien or a new chocolate digestive biscuit?' Both of them started to laugh so much they didn't notice Luke Whelan walking up behind them.

'Hi, did you enjoy the club?' he asked.

'It was great,' Belle answered.

'Brilliant!' Jazz enthused. 'I just wish we could join right now.'

'I was on the waiting list for nearly a year,' Luke told them.

'Nearly a year!' they squeaked but Luke wasn't listening. His eyes had strayed nervously to an older boy approaching them.

'Eh!' yelled the boy. 'Get over here.' Without a word of goodbye Luke left.

'Who was that?' Belle asked crossly.

'Seth Whelan, Luke's older brother,' Jazz said with a downward turn of her mouth. 'He's a bit of a bully.' They watched Luke slouch across the playground with his brother, looking quite unlike the nice, cheerful boy who'd shown them round the drama club at the weekend.

'Luke's the youngest of four boys,' Jazz continued. 'I know because they all came to this school and they were all nasty. The eldest used to enjoy picking on Jamal.'

'But Luke's great,' Belle said quickly.

'At the drama club maybe but he changes character when he's around his brothers. Probably has to,' Jazz added thoughtfully.

'Poor Luke,' Belle murmured, as she watched him noisily kicking a football round the school play-ground.

'Yes, we all have our problems,' Jazz added quietly.

On Friday morning Belle was late for school. As she scrabbled around in the hall cupboard under the stairs, searching for her school plimsolls and PE shorts, her dad called, 'Letter for you, Belle.'

With plimsolls on the brain Belle hardly heard him

and the letter he'd carefully left on the hall table was still waiting for her when she got back from school later that afternoon. At the sight of it Belle's heart started to pound. She snatched it up and opened it quickly. Yes! It was from the Cambridge Arts Centre. With her stomach doing triple somersaults she nervously scanned the page. Oh, please, *please* let it be the answer she'd been praying for. Suddenly her eyes lighted on the line, 'So if you'd like to be a Munchkin in our Christmas production we'd be delighted to have you.'

'YES!' she yelled, going up like a rocket. 'MUM! MUM! I'm going to be a Munchkin!'

Hearing the racket Belle's baby brother, Ben, toddled into the hall. 'I've got in!' cried Belle, sweeping him into her arms and waltzing him into the kitchen, singing a silly song: 'I've got into the Drama Club. I've got into the Drama Club.'

'Ben come too,' said the little boy.

'No way,' Belle replied as she carefully set him down on the kitchen floor. 'Ben goes to playgroup, Belle goes to drama club.'

'Absolutely,' agreed Mrs Forest. 'We don't want two dippy actors in the family.'

'Mum, can you believe it?' Belle cried.

'Not quite,' Mrs Forest answered. 'You said the club was full.'

'It was – it is!' Belle corrected herself. 'But Helen Powers —'

'Ooh, isn't she the actress in EastEnders?' Mrs Forest interrupted.

'Yes, and she runs the Children's Drama Club too – thousands of people want to go,' Belle continued dramatically. 'She's offered my friend and I a —'

'WHAT friend?' Mrs Forest interrupted again.

'Yasmin Khan, from school,' Belle answered, impatient to get back to her letter. 'Listen to this.' She read out loud: ' "So if you'd like to be a Munchkin in our Christmas production we'd be delighted to have you. Please come along to rehearsal on Saturday at two o'clock." '

'Munchkin?' Mrs Forest muttered, completely unimpressed.

Belle wondered why she ever started the conversation with her mother. Experience should have taught her by now that her mum always got the wrong end of the stick because she never listened to the important details, just the silly ones!

'Munchkins in *The Wizard of Oz*,' she explained crossly.

'Oh! You're going to be in a play,' Mrs Forest exclaimed, as the penny finally dropped. 'What about your homework?'

Belle couldn't believe she was hearing right. Here she was making her stage debut and her mum was fretting about homework! She kept her cool, though, and answered calmly.

'It's not much work. Just a few songs and some dancing.'

A flicker of anxiety crossed Mrs Forest's face. 'Remember, Belle,' she warned. 'You've not to neglect your schoolwork. You were top of the class for two years running in Manchester and we're hoping you'll do just as well here in Cambridge. They're a brighter lot at the Charles Darwin,' she added sharply. 'So you'll have to work harder just to keep up, you know.'

Belle nodded. She would have agreed to walk the plank and swim the Atlantic chased by girl-eating sharks just so long as she got to go to the drama club.

'It's a deal, mum,' she answered.

'It had better be,' Mrs Forest replied.

Fortunately Ben's neglected baked beans began to burn on the stove and Mrs Forest quickly turned her attention to them. Sighing with relief Belle dashed out of the kitchen and into the hall where she dialled Jazz's number.

'62462,' said Jamal.

'Er, er, hello,' she spluttered. 'Is Jazz there?'

'Yes, hold on,' he answered politely. 'I'll get her.'

Belle heard Jamal call out for Jazz then she heard Jazz thunder downstairs like a charging elephant. There was a scrunching noise, as if she was grabbing the phone and squeezing it hard, then a loud squeak.

'I'm a Munchkin!' yelled Jazz.

'So am I,' cried Belle.

'Isn't it brilliant,' Jazz raved. 'We're in the drama club Christmas show!' She quickly dropped her voice, just in case somebody was listening. 'Do you think we're *actually* in the drama club or do you think when the Christmas show's over we'll be given the boot?'

'Who knows?' Belle answered cheerfully. 'Let's just enjoy what we've got.'

'Yes, you're right,' Jazz agreed. 'Though I do have a little family problem.'

'Oh, no. Not again.'

'I'll have to dream up some big excuse, fast,' Jazz added tensely.

'You *must*, Jazz,' Belle insisted. 'I can't be a

Munchkin without you. Who would I have to laugh with?'

'Tracie Long, the Wicked Witch of the East,' Jazz teased. Belle laughed but she was worried. Getting into the drama club Christmas play would be no joy without Jazz right there in the chorus line beside her.

CHAPTER FOUR
★
On Stage

Saturday dawned and instead of feeling happy and excited Belle felt tense and anxious. Would Jazz make it to the drama club?

'You don't look very happy,' Mr Forest teased as Belle picked at her lunch. 'What's wrong, has acting taken away your lifelong passion for pizzas?'

'No, I'm just a bit nervous,' she replied.

'You, nervous?' he laughed. 'Now that's a novel experience.'

'Oh, Dad, stop winding me up,' Belle begged.

'Sorry, love,' said Mr Forest, cheerfully helping himself to her rejected pizza. 'I thought you'd be cock-a-hoop at the thought of getting into the drama club.'

'I am,' she insisted.

Suddenly the front door bell rang.

'I'll get it,' said Belle, gratefully jumping up from the table. When she opened the door Jazz was standing there, looking very hot and bothered.

'What's happened?' Belle asked.

'I —' Jazz started but stopped as Mrs Forest walked into the hall.

'Mum, this is my friend, Jazz,' Belle said.

'Pleased to meet you,' said Mrs Forest warmly. 'Come in.' Belle led Jazz into the dining-room where she introduced her to everybody. Jazz smiled and scooped up Ben.

'I've got a baby sister,' she told him. 'She's called Predeep.'

'I'm called Ben,' he answered very solemnly. 'I go to playgroup and Belle goes to drama club.'

'Me too,' laughed Jazz. 'Aren't we lucky?'

With the formalities over Belle whisked Jazz upstairs to her bedroom.

'So, come on, tell me what happened?' she asked as she firmly shut her bedroom door.

'My parents asked me umpteen awkward questions. Where I was going, who with, etcetera, etcetera,' Jazz explained. 'It all got pretty tricky.'

'I don't want to add to your worries but you've got to do something, you know,' said Belle, sitting on the bed beside Jazz. 'You just can't go on lying through your teeth every weekend.'

'I hardly told a single lie,' Jazz remonstrated. 'That

was the problem, sticking to the truth but not actually saying where I was going.'

'You need a foolproof excuse that will get you out of the house every Saturday afternoon, no questions asked,' Belle said thoughtfully.

'The truth would be the best thing of all,' Jazz said. 'I'm sick of deceiving them, and I'm no good at it either.'

'We'll have to come up with something,' said Belle with a smile. 'Otherwise we'll both be so stressed out we won't be able to perform properly!'

Seeing the time on her bedside table she leaped up and threw open her wardrobe doors. 'Now what shall I wear?' she said desperately.

Half an hour later clothes were all over the floor and both girls were standing in front of the mirror inspecting themselves.

'I wish I had trendy clothes like the older girls at the drama club,' Belle moaned.

'I always look so boring!' grumbled Jazz as she stared at herself in the mirror. 'Tall and thin with scraggy hair!'

'Rubbish!' cried Belle. 'You look better than me. My feet are too big and my stomach's fat!' The girls started to laugh at each other's list of complaints.

'We'd better stop moaning,' said Jazz. 'Or we'll be late for our première!'

They cycled across Midsummer Common with the wild November wind tearing at the trees, scattering leaves and conkers on to the footpaths. Belle jumped off her bike and grabbed a handful of the shiny-new conkers.

'For Ben,' she said. 'He's conkers bonkers!'

'You're conkers bonkers,' laughed Jazz. 'Come on!'

They arrived at the Drama Centre windswept but on time.

'Hey! You're back,' Luke called in surprise. Both girls nodded happily.

'Helen asked us to come along and fill out the Munchkin chorus line,' Belle explained.

'Good,' said Daisy. 'It was looking very thin last week.' Belle liked Daisy immediately. She was pretty and talented but not at all big-headed. Quite unlike Tracie Long who was strutting round the hall like Madonna at an autograph signing session.

'Right,' said Helen, clapping her hands for quiet. 'You don't have to be a mathematician to work out how many rehearsal Saturdays we've got left.'

'Not enough!' Jerome yelled.

'Exactly,' Helen agreed. 'So I want you in next

weekend, for two full days, ten till four if you can manage it?' All eighteen eagerly nodded. 'Good. Check it out with your parents. I don't want angry phone calls from those whose children forget to tell them,' Helen added. 'Before we warm up, I've recruited Belle and Jazz for Munchkins. Come on, girls, you'll need to loosen up too.'

They didn't need asking twice. In a flash they joined the circle and did some breathing exercises, then after a few light warm-ups, Helen split them into two groups. Belle and Jazz stayed close to the twins and Daisy so that they could be in the same group.

'This game is called "Adverbs",' said Helen, 'I want one group to think of an action, nothing rude or anything to do with toilets!' she added with a knowing smile. 'And the other group will tell them how to do it; quickly, slowly, angrily, arrogantly – whatever, but then they must guess what the action is. Off you go.'

Belle's group decided their action was going to be 'dancing at a disco'. The second group, led by Luke, then told them to do it 'snootily'.

'How do you disco-dance snootily?' Jazz giggled as they stood up.

'I don't know, but here goes!' laughed Belle as she pranced all over the room, wriggling her bottom and shaking her legs. Eventually Luke's group guessed what their action was, then they switched around. It was their turn to do the action, which was 'milking a cow', and Belle's group told them to do it 'in slow motion'. It was a madly funny half-hour and nobody seemed to mind how silly they looked. Even Tracie Long forgot her self-importance as she mimed riding a horse angrily! By the end of it Belle and Jazz were laughing so much they ached. Helen did a couple of rounds of Simple Simon, followed by a brief five-minute break, which gave them just enough time to nip to the loo and grab a cold drink, then on with 'the show', as Helen called rehearsals.

Belle and Jazz leaped up on to the stage, rapidly followed by Millie and Rozzie.

'I thought you were Glinda, the Good Witch of the West?' Belle said to Rozzie.

'I am, but when I'm not Glinda I'm a Munchkin!' Rozzie explained.

'Watch out for Elvira the pianist, she's a bit of a dragon if you miss your cue,' Millie warned.

'But we don't even know the songs,' Jazz gulped nervously.

'Don't worry, just hum!' Rozzie answered. 'She'll be

nice to *you* because you're new. It's us lot that will get the grief.'

Elvira swanned in, this week dressed entirely in purple and emerald green.

'Love her colour sense,' said Millie behind her hand.

Jazz snorted and pressed her hankie over her face to cover her laughter. Elvira looked at Jazz then asked grandly. 'Are you sick, child?' Jazz shook her head and straightened her face.

'No, just a tickly throat,' she fibbed.

'Well get rid of it, darling. I need clear, sweet voices. Ah-ah-ah-ah-ah!' she sang as she ran up and down the scales. Both girls gaped at her in amazement.

'Come along, where are your song sheets?' she demanded.

'Here,' said Belle, flapping her sheet. 'But we don't know them yet.'

'I'll give you a week to learn, no more,' said Elvira. 'Other Munchkins,' she said, fixing the rest of the chorus with a beady eye, 'I expect you word perfect today, and no dithering around on your cues. Off we go!' With an elegant flourish Elvira's plump little hands hit the keyboard and the opening chords of 'Somewhere over the Rainbow' filled the hall.

'One, two, three, four,' she cried, counting Daisy in on the beats. Daisy opened her mouth and sang like a bird. Belle's skin prickled at the beauty of her voice and her eyes filled with tears as she listened to the girl singing with such sadness and longing.

' "Somewhere over the rainbow, bluebirds fly. Birds fly over the rainbow, why then, oh, why, can't I?" '

The opening scene was swiftly followed by the Kansas tornado scene, where Dorothy and Toto, the little black Scottie dog, are whisked away by the 'twister'.

'We'll have thunder, lightning and howling wind,' Helen explained to Daisy. 'Then the stage will go black and you'll wake up in the beautiful land of Oz. OK, give it a whirl, Daisy. From the moment you wake up.'

Because the lighting and sounds effects would all be added at a later date Helen had to make all the noises herself, including bluebirds softly chirruping! Clutching Toto, who for the moment was a rolled-up sweatshirt, Daisy peeped out of her door and came face to face with a huddle of Munchkins, all staring in at her. They whispered in high, squeaky voices which made Belle want to giggle but she tried hard not to. No way was this a joke. She and Jazz were lucky having

Rozzie and Millie close by. They copied their every move as they skipped back and forth across the stage singing, ' "We're off to see the wizard, the wonderful wizard of Oz." '

While Dorothy was doing her scenes with the Scarecrow, the Munchkins waited backstage.

'Don't touch a thing,' Millie whispered, pointing at the rows of knobs and levers. 'Or you might bring the lights down on Daisy's head!'

Belle wouldn't have dreamed of touching anything. She was perfectly happy just being there, smiling into the warm darkness. This was *living*! Acting was no longer a pipe dream but something all around her. She could see it, smell it, touch it, be it!

The rehearsal time flashed by far too quickly. When Helen called 'Time's up, everybody. Thank you' Belle felt like bursting into tears. She adored being there. Loved it! The last thing she wanted to do was leave and return to the world of ordinary events, like going home, doing homework and watching television.

'I wish I could live here,' she muttered to Rozzie.

'What as, the theatre mouse?' Rozzie giggled.

'You did excellently, girls,' Helen said as she walked over to Belle and Jazz. 'I don't think I've ever seen two

51

happier Munchkins.' The girls beamed with pleasure. 'Have you got your song sheets?' she asked.

'Yes, and Elvira says we've got to learn them by next week,' Belle replied.

'Is that a problem?' Helen asked. Both girls shook their heads.

'No, we'll practise them together,' Belle replied.

'Well don't give your parents earache, will you?' Helen teased. 'Can you make two full rehearsal days next weekend?' she added.

'Yes,' they answered together but Belle could hear a hint of doubt in Jazz's voice. We've got to do something to sort out this mess, she thought. Little did she know that her mother had already set the ball in motion.

CHAPTER FIVE

★

Home Truths

Belle got home in the pouring rain, starving hungry and blissfully happy. As she devoured her mum's delicious lasagne she chatted non-stop about the drama club and the fun they'd had.

'I see you've got your appetite back,' teased Mr Forest. 'Was it fun?'

'Magic!' Belle exclaimed.

'Oh, by the way,' her mum said absently. 'While you were out Jazz's mum phoned. Mrs Khan, I think she said?'

Belle swallowed her forkful of food the wrong way and nearly choked. As her dad patted her on the back she spluttered, 'Did you tell her where Jazz and I were this afternoon?'

Unaware of the bomb she'd exploded in the Khan household, Mrs Forest said casually, 'Yes, of course. She seemed anxious so I said you'd both gone to the drama club and would be back about five-thirty.' Seeing the horror written clear across Belle's face she added, with a penetrating gaze, 'Did Jazz actually tell her parents where she was going?'

Belle hesitated, wondering whether it was easier to go for a white lie or tell the truth. Seeing the mess Jazz was in as a result of her half lies Belle decided it was best to go for the simple truth.

'No,' she said and braced herself for an angry reaction. Oddly enough it didn't come.

'That explains why Mrs Khan turned peculiar over the phone,' Mrs Forest said thoughtfully.

Mr Forest, who had the habit of always hitting the nail right on the head, said, 'So what's the problem?'

'They're Bengali,' Jazz answered.

'That's not a problem,' her dad pointed out.

'It is if you want to make acting your career,' Belle explained.

'Well, I'm not Bengali but I think it's the daftest career in the world!' said her mum.

'Shh,' said Mr Forest. 'Let's hear what Belle has to say.'

Already regretting that she'd ever started the conversation Belle kept the details to the barest minimum.

'They're Muslims and they don't want their daughter on stage. They think Jazz should be a scientist, like her big brother.' Belle wriggled, uncomfortably aware that was exactly what her parents wanted for her.

Mrs Forest bristled in sympathy but her dad stayed more objective.

'It's a hard career to follow at the best of times,' Mr Forest said thoughtfully. 'But especially hard in Jazz's situation.'

'Dad!' Belle cried. 'Jazz is a brilliant actress. She's got real talent and she loves acting. What she's supposed to do – ignore it?'

'No,' he answered calmly. 'Jazz has a lot to sort out and we should help her if we can.'

'How?' Belle asked, bewildered.

'She'll tell you,' he answered wisely.

Belle's thoughts were with Jazz all weekend but she didn't dare phone her at home, just in case she made things worse, and Jazz didn't phone her either. When they met up at school on Monday morning Jazz's face was pale and she had dark circles under her eyes.

'I'm sorry,' Belle said, 'My mum dropped you in it good and proper.'

'Not really,' Jazz answered. 'My parents would have found out sooner or later. Jamal's right. They're not stupid. It's me that's stupid, thinking I can get away with deceiving them.'

The whistle went and the girls hurried into class for double maths. Double maths, on a Monday morning – the lesson from hell! At playtime they had a little longer to talk but got interrupted by Luke.

'Hi,' he called cheerfully. 'Good on Saturday, wasn't it?'

'Brilliant,' Belle answered. Jazz just nodded.

'Gone off the boil have you?' Luke asked her. Jazz crinkled up her brow. 'What?'

'Gone off drama club, have you?' he persisted. It was all Jazz needed. She shook her head and burst into tears.

'Blimey,' Luke gasped as he turned to Belle. 'I never meant to upset her.' Checking that nobody was watching he tentatively put a hand on Jazz's shuddering back and patted her gently.

'I love the club,' Jazz sobbed. 'It's my parents, they don't want me to go.' Luke's expression turned to genuine sympathy.

'If you've got troubles at home I'm the one to speak to,' he said as he led the girls to a quiet corner of the playground. 'I'm the *expert*!' he added with a bitter laugh.

Belle and Jazz gaped at him, nonplussed. 'You!' they said together.

'Why?' Jazz cried. 'You're a boy. In my house being a boy is a *big* plus.'

'Not in mine,' Luke replied. 'I'm one of four, and I'm the youngest.'

Jazz struggled to find the right words so as not to offend Luke. 'You're very different to your older brothers,' she said cautiously.

'You mean I'm not a bully?' he asked, bluntly.

Jazz nodded. 'One of your brothers used to pick on my brother, Jamal,' she told him awkwardly.

'That'd be Jake, he's a big bully. I should know, he practises a lot on me,' he added grimly. 'Still, I'm sorry he gave your brother a hard time.'

'Don't your mum and dad ever catch him at it?' Belle asked, red with indignation. Too late she felt Jazz's elbow dig her in the ribs.

'My dad's dead,' Luke answered without a quiver of emotion. 'Died when I was a baby.'

'Oh . . . I'm sorry,' Belle murmured, furious with herself for being so stupid.

Luke shrugged. 'It was a long time ago. I hardly remember him.'

'So who gives you grief about the drama club?' Jazz persisted, clearly fascinated. 'Your mum?'

'No way,' Luke replied. 'She's cool. It's my brothers. They think acting's for girls.'

'Funny,' said Jazz. 'My parents think acting is only for boys. We should swop families,' she joked.

Luke shook his head. 'No, you wouldn't like my lot. Funny thing is, my dad used to be an entertainer.'

'What?' the girls cried, impressed.

'He was a comedian, in the clubs, one of the best mimics in the business, I'm told,' he said proudly.

'So are you,' Jazz enthused. 'You must have inherited his talent. What about the other boys, are they comics too?'

Luke shook his head. 'No way. They think standing up in public pretending to be somebody else is a waste of time. If they ever found out I'd joined the drama club they'd have my guts for garters!'

'Then you mustn't let them find out,' Jazz replied vehemently.

'They have a way of making everything their business,' Luke said.

'How?' Jazz asked.

'Easy. They just open all my letters,' Luke told her. Seeing Jazz's gloomy face he added, 'You've got to persuade your parents to let you do at least this term at the drama club.'

'A term!' she cried. 'Dream on.'

'Make a deal,' he insisted. 'Tell them you'll stop lying if they'll trust you. Tell them they can come along with you and check it out for themselves —'

'No way!' Jazz cried, her eyes flashing.

'Cool it,' Luke said, laughing at her indignant face. 'I don't mean they should stay *all* day. Just pop in, give it the once over, then go. Once they know what you're up to they might stop fretting.'

'That makes sense to me,' Belle chipped in.

'But they'll be so embarrassing,' Jazz wailed.

'All parents are embarrassing,' Belle pointed out.

'Do you really think they would just look round, then go?' Jazz said, still worried by the suggestion.

'Sure,' Luke answered with confidence.

'That's good advice,' Belle added. 'I hope you'll take it.'

'I will,' Jazz said. 'I promise.'

CHAPTER SIX

★

Straight Talking

The next morning Belle was at school so early she surprised herself, but there was one person there, even before her, and that was Luke.

'You're an early bird,' she teased.

'I don't hang about at home,' he explained. 'Too much earache. Know what I mean?' Belle smiled sympathetically.

'I wanted to get here early so I could find out if Jazz had talked to her parents,' Belle admitted.

'We can ask her,' Luke said. 'Here she comes now.'

Jazz came running down the road, her wonderful hair streaming out behind her in a dark, silky cloud.

'What happened?' Belle cried, pouncing on her. 'Did you speak to your mum and dad?'

Jazz beamed and nodded.

'I certainly did,' she said, very pleased with herself. 'Just before I went to bed I said I knew I'd deceived them, but that was because I was frightened of telling them the truth and worrying them. They think the drama club's no good so I asked them to come and check it out for themselves. I'll introduce them to

60

Helen and all my friends and then they can make their own decision!' Jazz stopped for breath, her topaz-yellow eyes sparkling. 'What about that then?'

'I'm impressed,' smiled Luke.

'What did they say?' Belle cried.

'They just about fell off the sofa,' Jazz said, bursting into peals of laughter. 'It was the last thing they expected.'

'So they're coming?' Belle asked astonished.

'Yes,' Jazz answered.

'I told you it would work,' Luke said triumphantly.

'It did, though they'd still have a heart attack if they ever saw me on stage,' Jazz pointed out.

'Then be sure to get them out of the hall before we start the *Oz* rehearsals,' Luke said. 'Just let them see us doing our warm-ups and playing games, then usher them gently towards the exit signs.'

Jazz grimaced. 'I've got to admit, the thought of them being there makes me die.'

'Come on. When we're into our drama a herd of elephants could charge through and none of us would even notice,' Luke laughed.

Belle spent the next few days going around the house singing at the top of her voice.

'Put a sock in it, Belle,' her sister Claire bellowed as she hollered 'Over the Rainbow' in the shower.

Mr Forest, who played the piano beautifully and sang really well too, suggested he accompany Belle on the piano. So every night before bed they'd go through the song sheets together and by the end of the week everybody, even baby Ben, was going around the house humming tunes from the play.

'You're much better than you were, Belle,' Claire remarked.

'Yes, she's got a sweet voice,' her father said proudly. 'My little songbird,' he added, tousling Belle's hair like he used to do when she was a toddler.

By Saturday Belle was nearly word perfect and sang all the way across the common to the Library Theatre. As she locked up her bike outside the library Belle spotted Jazz hurrying up the steps, followed by her parents. They looked much younger than Belle had imagined. Mrs Khan was small and slender with a lovely face, exactly like Jazz's. She wore a ruby silk sari, trimmed with a gold filigree pattern round the edges, and carried herself with grace and elegance. Mr Khan was very tall and rather thin, with raven-dark hair and large, gentle eyes. Belle hung back, not sure what to do, but Jazz spotted her and beamed with relief.

'Hi!' she yelled as she waited for Belle to catch up. 'This is my very best friend, Belle Forest,' Jazz said. 'These are my parents,' she added shyly. The Khans smiled warmly.

'I spoke to your mother the other day,' Mrs Khan said. 'I hope she didn't mind me ringing. I was so worried about Jazz. I'd no idea where she was, you see.'

Belle shook her head. 'She didn't mind at all.'

They chatted all the way up the four flights to the theatre, where Jazz pushed open the doors and ushered them in.

'Goodness, it's very grand,' said her dad, clearly impressed by the stylish foyer and the comfortable waiting area with its colour co-ordinated sofas and coffee tables.

'Only the best for us rising stars,' said Jazz grandly.

When they walked into the hall there were children everywhere, on stage, off stage, singing, dancing, painting props, trying on costumes, or just messing about! Luke was right, though. Nobody cared who came in; in fact they hardly noticed the unexpected arrival of Jazz's parents. But Helen immediately spotted them and came over to introduce herself.

'How very nice to see you both,' she said, shaking Mr and Mrs Khan firmly by the hand.

'Thank you for letting us come,' Mrs Khan answered politely, her eyes sweeping round the room, taking in every single detail. 'I see you're preparing for a show?'

'Yes,' Helen replied cheerily. 'We always put on a Christmas show. It's great fun for everybody, especially us,' she said with a winning smile. 'Come and meet some of my students.' Belle could see Jazz visibly sighing with relief as Helen led her parents away from the stage, towards a group of older girls and boys stitching sequins on to curtains that were part of the Munchkin set.

'Good move,' Jazz whispered as they trailed after Helen. 'Keep their minds on the backstage work.'

Suddenly there was a loud squeak from the stage. 'Help!' called Millie.

When Rozzie stepped out of the wings, her feet were the brightest yellow. Everybody stopped what they were doing and stared in horror, then burst into laughter.

'What happened?' cried Helen, dashing over to help.

'I was hopping about and my foot accidentally landed in the paint pot and knocked it over,' Rozzie explained, near to tears.

'Quick,' said Helen to an older boy. 'Get the turpentine.'

Before anybody could move Mr Khan grabbed the turps bottle and a rag, then leaped on stage and cleaned Rozzie's feet in no time.

'Oh, thank you,' she cried, relieved that she wasn't going to have yellow feet for the rest of her life.

'No problem,' said Mr Khan, wiping his smeared hands on the turps rag. 'I suggest you go and wash your feet in soap and water to get rid of the smell.'

Rozzie dashed off, followed by Millie, and Mr Khan set about cleaning up the stage.

'No, no, let me,' insisted Helen.

'Why should two of us have yellow hands?' Mr Khan reasoned. 'Mine are already dirty.'

Nevertheless Helen got down on her knees beside Mr Khan and together they cleaned up the stage, leaving Mrs Khan with the sewing group, showing them a quick, clever way to hand-sew rows of sequins.

'Do you think they're going to stay all day?' Jazz fretted.

'No, but I think they're brilliant!' Belle replied 'They're SO nice.' Jazz glowed with pleasure.

'They are quite sweet at times,' she admitted.

Suddenly they heard Mrs Khan saying to Jerome, who was sitting beside her stitching sequins, 'Are you in the play?'

'I'm the Lion,' he answered with a grin.

'That sounds very impressive,' she replied.

'Not really,' Jerome said. 'I'm not a brave lion, I'm scared of everything.'

Mrs Khan laughed at his explanation. 'It sounds fun,' she said.

'You should come and see the play,' Jerome urged. 'We're all in it.'

Jazz's fingers gripped Belle's arm like a vice. 'If she finds out I'm a Munchkin I'm history,' she muttered. Luckily Helen called the group together.

'OK, now that we've finished painting the stage yellow we can get on with the show,' she joked.

Mr and Mrs Khan whispered their goodbyes and headed quietly for the door.

'Aren't you staying?' Helen asked.

'No, no,' Mr Khan replied. 'We've taken up quite

enough of your time. Thank you very much for letting us look round. It's been most interesting.' Mrs Khan nodded in agreement.

'Thank you,' she added. 'Goodbye.'

Jazz waved goodbye, then caught Luke's knowing grin.

'I told you so,' he mouthed across the circle at her.

'Warming-up exercises first,' Helen said, shaking herself all over, like a dog. 'Loosen up, guys, we've got a lot of hard work ahead and I want those muscles warm and soft.'

They jumped up and down on the spot, hopping and skipping before Helen called out, 'Split up into pairs. One hand behind your back and let's see some flourishing one-armed sword fencing!'

They all loved Helen's crazy games and laughed themselves silly doing them but there was always method in Helen's play. After ten minutes of one-armed fencing the group were warm, loose and very relaxed.

'Now for a spot of Museums,' called Helen. 'Four in a group this time. Decide on a statue pose. One of you be the nose, the other the bottom, the third the head and the fourth the knee-caps.' Jazz, Millie, Rozzie and Belle decided to do a statue of Donald Duck. The twins were a laugh at the best of times but making a statue of Donald Duck they were hysterical! Neither of them could move for giggling so Jazz took control and shoved them into position.

'You be Donald's head,' she said to Millie. 'I'll do his beak and Rozzie can do his knees.'

'Great,' said Belle. 'That leaves me as the rear end!' She stuck out her bottom as far as it would go, and Jazz at the other end put both of her hands together, opening and closing them like a beak.

'Q-U-A-C-K!' she honked like a duck in pain.

Shaking with laughter the four girls managed to hold their position long enough for Helen to inspect them.

'What on earth is this?' she said as she puzzled over their knotted tangle of arms and legs. 'An octopus?'

This time Jazz managed to improve her sound effects.

'QUACK-QUACK-Q-U-A-C-K!' she went.

'Donald Duck,' called Luke as the girls tumbled to the floor.

After the physical warm-ups it was time to give their voices an airing.

'Hold your noses,' said Helen. 'Hold them tight

and sing yin-yin-yin-yin, until you run out of breath.' The racket that followed was tremendous.

'Yin-yin-yin-yin!' they chanted.

'Enough,' cried Helen over the clamour. 'That's loosened up one part of your face and throat, now let's try other parts. Imagine I've just given you the most gi-nor-mous toffee in the world. Watch me.'

Helen opened her mouth as wide as was humanly possible and crammed in an imaginary toffee. She started chewing it, twisting and turning her mouth and jaw as she sucked and chomped on the toffee.

'Your turn,' she said, letting her face fall back into its normal lines. 'Don't overdo it and get lockjaw!'

It was a fun exercise and useful too. As Belle chewed on her imaginary toffee she could feel her jaw relax and her cheek muscles loosen up.

'Finally,' said Helen. 'A few interesting tongue-twisters, to sing in any key you choose. Start with this one – fluffy floppy puppy,' she sang in a high chanting voice. The group sang too, some high, some low, some in a long drone.

'Fluffy floppy puppy. Fluffy floppy puppy,' echoed loud around the room.

'Now change to cracked cricket critic,' Helen called. The wailing and squawking as all eighteen sang in different pitches was terrible but at least they'd loosened up their voice boxes.

'Good, now on with the show, from the top,' said Helen.

Belle and Jazz fell in line beside Rozzie and Millie as Elvira, this week in black and white, hit the piano keys for the opening song. Daisy's wonderful voice soared and dipped to the music of 'Somewhere over the Rainbow'. As Scene One got underway the chorus slipped backstage where they were supposed to wait quietly for their cue. No such behaviour was possible in the chaotic company of Rozzie and Millie. One of them got wrapped up in the stage curtain, the other tripped over a length of cable and landed on her bottom in the prop basket! Jazz and Belle covered their mouths, trying to suppress their giggles, but Helen still heard them.

'Shut up back there!' she shouted.

Everybody did until Luke popped up in the wings wearing his scarecrow hat and straw gloves.

'Here comes Worzel Gummidge,' sniggered Rozzie. Luke tickled her with his long, spiky, straw fingers but fortunately her laughter was covered by Helen's tornado sound effects. They all jumped when

Helen bashed a drum for the thunder sound effects; then everything went pitch-dark.

'Spoo-kee!' whispered Luke.

As the lights came slowly up they lit the stage all the colours of the rainbow and the sound effects were of soft warbling birds and gently splashing water.

'It's like fairyland,' Belle said, in a dreamy voice.

'It *is* fairyland,' hissed Jazz. 'It's over the rainbow and we should have a cue any minute now.'

When they heard their cue the Munchkins scampered on stage singing 'Ding-Dong, the Witch is Dead'.

Belle loved all the songs, not just her own but everybody else's too! Dorothy's, the Scarecrow's, the Lion's and the Tin Man's. In fact there wasn't a song in the show that she didn't now know off by heart. She hummed every single one under her breath or sang them out loud when she thought nobody could overhear her.

'Talk about songs on the brain,' Luke said as he passed Belle backstage. 'Do you ever stop singing?'

'Only when I'm asleep,' she laughed.

At the end of the day Helen called Belle over for a chat. 'How's it going?' she asked.

'Great,' Belle answered. 'I've had a brilliant time.'

'Good,' Helen replied. 'I've been listening to you singing,' she added.

Belle blushed bright red and wondered if she was going to get a ticking-off for humming backstage.

'You've got a good strong voice,' said Helen.

'I wish it was like Daisy's,' Belle sighed. 'She sings like a real professional.'

'Everybody's different,' Helen replied evenly. 'You have a good memory, too. You seem to know all the songs,' she said with a smile.

Belle nodded. 'I do,' she admitted. 'I'm driving my family mad.'

'Well, I've been thinking,' said Helen. 'I've got to find an understudy for Daisy. Heaven forbid that she should suddenly fall ill but these things do happen in the theatre. Would you like to understudy her?'

'Me!' squeaked Belle. 'Me, play Dorothy?'

'Well, only if Daisy's ill,' Helen quickly added.

Belle gulped hard and tried hard to steady her breath.

'Yes, I'd love to,' she answered, her pale blue eyes wide with excitement.

'Excellent,' said Helen. 'I'll tell Daisy and get you a copy of the script. I hope you won't need it but it's better to be safe than sorry in this business.' And she went off leaving an astounded Belle.

'Yoo-hoo! What planet are we on?' Jazz teased as she passed by and saw Belle's starstruck expression.

'Jazz,' Belle whispered like somebody waking from a dream. 'Helen's just asked me to understudy Daisy.'

'Wow!' Jazz gasped.

'It's amazing,' Belle replied.

'Then smile instead of looking so stunned,' Jazz said.

'I am stunned – flabbergasted!' Belle replied, then hurriedly added, 'But I'd hate anything horrible to happen to Daisy. She's so good and I'm just ordinary.'

'Good or not, if Daisy got a bad cold or lost her voice during a performance we'd all be in a pickle without an understudy,' Jazz reminded her.

'Yes,' Belle agreed as she slowly started to smile. 'The best thing about understudying Daisy is that I get to wear the Wicked Witch of the East's magic shoes.'

'Ugh! I bet Tracie Long's feet really pong!' laughed Jazz.

CHAPTER SEVEN

★

Understudy

The next day, Sunday, was the extra rehearsal day. It was strange getting up early and cycling over Midsummer Common, empty apart from a few pigeons and a stray dog, with the church bells ringing out across the city.

It was a hectic morning with only a five minute break, then lunch at one o'clock. Belle and Jazz were tucking into their sandwiches when Daisy joined them.

'I hear you're going to be understudying me,' she said to Belle with a smile.

'Yes,' Belle replied self-consciously. 'Helen asked if I would.'

'Thank goodness!' said Daisy, opening her smart red leather rucksack. 'It's a load off my mind. Want a cheese and cucumber sandwich?' she said, holding out a pack of daintily-cut sandwiches.

'Yes please,' both girls said eagerly, and in exchange for a round of Daisy's wholemeal sandwiches they gave her a Peperami and a packet of salt and vinegar crisps.

'Mmm, this is the best lunch I've ever had here,' said Daisy. 'It's so much nicer when you share things, don't you think?'

Belle's mouth was too full of food to answer but she nodded in agreement as she gazed at Daisy. With her lovely red-gold hair and silver-grey eyes she really was the prettiest girl Belle had ever seen – and she wore great clothes too! Today she had on a really nice blue-and-white stretch tee shirt under a pair of soft denim dungarees. Best thing of all were her trendy black Kicker boots, the exact ones Belle had been longing for. Belle reckoned the whole outfit must have come to at least a hundred pounds. Her limit at any one shopping spree was twenty pounds, so it was either a pair of shoes, a dress, or jeans. Never all of them together! The resulting fashion look constantly irritated Belle. One thing would be just right and everything else would be slightly out of date. Sighing she rallied her thoughts and listened to what Daisy was saying.

'You see, sometimes I'm not absolutely sure I can make it to the drama club,' she said.

'Why?' Belle asked.

Daisy looked at Belle's puzzled face and said, slowly and reluctantly, 'My father doesn't know I come here every Saturday. If he knew he'd go mad and ground me – for ever! So I have to be very careful.'

Belle gulped. This was serious news indeed. No wonder Helen was keen to get Daisy an understudy.

'My mum's completely supportive,' Daisy quickly added. 'She's explained everything to Helen. It's Dad who's against the notion of me going on stage.'

Belle and Jazz looked at each other, as if to say 'not another!'

'So what do you do?' asked Jazz, instantly sympathetic.

'My mum covers for me,' Daisy answered. 'She's always let me act. Even as a little kid she'd give me clothes to dress up in and we'd sing and dance together. The minute Dad walked in we used to stop.'

Belle couldn't believe what she was hearing. What with Luke's bullying brothers, Jazz's mum and dad, and now Daisy's tyrannical father, the list of domestic problems was growing daily.

'So how come you're here?' asked Jazz, deeply intrigued.

'Well, my mum has a close friend who's quite a famous actress,' Daisy explained. 'This all sounds a bit big-headed,' she added with a blush. 'But she told Mum that I had talent and that's what made Mum decide to bring me here. We've been sneaking behind Dad's back for nearly a year.'

'Gosh! It must be hard for your mum, deceiving your dad,' said Jazz with real feeling.

Daisy nodded. 'I dread to think what my dad would do if he ever found out. That's why having Belle as my understudy takes the pressure off me – and Mum too,' she added.

'Well, I hope you're not off too much,' said Belle nervously.

Suddenly Luke appeared beside them.

'Just thought I'd warn you that Tracie Long's on the warpath! She's hopping mad that Belle's under-studying you, Daisy.'

'W-H-A-T?' cried Daisy, flabbergasted. 'How can she understudy me *and* play the Wicked Witch of the East?'

'Don't ask me,' Luke laughed. 'She's bananas! Thinks she can do *everything* ten times better than everybody else.'

'Oh no,' groaned Belle. 'That's all I need. Tracie Long breathing down my neck for the next few weeks.'

'Just thought I'd warn you,' said Luke. 'She's nasty

at the best of times but when she's jealous . . . Ugh,'
he shuddered dramatically, 'she's *mean*!'

Two hours later Belle discovered just how mean
Tracie Long could be. She was standing backstage
with the Munchkins, waiting for their cue to go on,
when she felt a sharp jab in her ribs.

'Ouch!' she yelped.

'So how come *you*, the new girl, gets to understudy
the lead part?' Tracie's voice hissed through the darkness.

'Why don't you ask Helen,' Belle hissed back, trying
to keep her angry voice as low as possible.

'Don't you worry, I will!' Tracie snarled. 'We all
think you've been smarming your way into Helen's
favour.'

'That's not true!' seethed Belle.

'Oh no?' sneered Tracie. 'First you and your friend
turn up to watch, then you invite yourself back as
Munchkins, and now you're understudying Daisy. For
a creep who can't act you're moving fast.'

Turning on her heel Tracie stalked off, leaving
Belle shaking all over. When their cue came to go on
stage Jazz had to give her a push from behind.

'Come, on Belle. Tracie's just trying to undermine

your confidence,' Jazz whispered. 'Don't let her beat you down, get a grip.'

Belle nodded and took a deep breath.

'No way is she going to win,' she said, and putting on her brightest Munchkin smile she ran on stage, dancing and singing like the happiest girl in the world.

It was a tricky afternoon, and a tiring one too, with lots of retakes and fiddly cues on and off stage to get right. During the final break, while Helen was in the foyer making a couple of phone calls, Karl, who played the Tin Man, suddenly started shouting at Luke.

'I'm fed up with you butting in and stealing the show.'

'What are you talking about?' Luke angrily retorted.

'You think you're everybody,' Karl snapped. 'Showing off and playing for all the laughs.'

'I'm saying the lines just like you are,' Luke reasoned. 'What do you want me to do – not say them at all?'

'I want you to stop hogging the show,' Karl said as he moved menacingly towards Luke.

'Come on, man,' Jerome interrupted. 'Luke *is* only playing his part.'

Belle and Jazz breathed a sigh of relief.

'Karl won't thump Luke if Jerome's on his side,' whispered Belle.

'The Scarecrow has a lot of good lines,' Jerome pointed out. 'It's not Luke's fault if they sound funny; they're meant to.'

Belle and Jazz stared at each other, astonished by Jerome's reasonable tone. From their first visit to the club they'd been terrified of this big, brooding giant with the ring in his nose but now they were seeing another side to him. This Jerome was a gentle peace-maker.

'My character must come over as a real softie,' Jerome continued. 'All the Lion ever does is snivel about how frightened he is. I can't change it, that's how he's written, but I can play it to the best of my ability.'

Karl's thunderous expression showed he wasn't one bit happy but he couldn't do a thing to Luke while Jerome was minding him. It was at that particularly touchy moment that Tracie Long decided to butt in.

'I think Karl's right,' she said in her loud, brassy

voice. 'Luke's always trying to upstage him. Pulling one of his funny faces or trying to get a quick laugh while Karl's speaking.'

'Yeah!' Karl agreed, angry all over again.

Fortunately Helen walked into the hall and the argument instantly stopped but everybody who'd heard it knew that it was only on hold. Karl, now publicly backed by Tracie, would definitely have another go at Luke, but not when Jerome Knight was within earshot.

CHAPTER EIGHT

★

Loyalty

Back at school Belle's head churned with thoughts of all kinds, some thrilling, some disturbing. Her excitement at being asked to understudy Daisy was edged with anxiety now that she knew just how sensitive Daisy's home situation was. What if Mr Belham-Thomas did ground his talented daughter? Was Belle really up to taking over the lead role? It was flattering to be asked but seriously terrifying too.

Then there was Luke. She and Jazz really liked him and felt sorry for the way he'd been attacked at the drama club. Hadn't he enough to put up with at home with his wretched brothers, without a hulk like Karl heavying him too? On Monday morning she and Jazz made it their business to say something to Luke just as soon as they found him alone in the playground.

'Yeah, it stinks,' he said gloomily. 'Drama club's always been the place where I could really relax, feel safe. Know what I mean?'

Both girls vigorously nodded their heads. They knew exactly what Luke was talking about.

'Now, just thinking about it makes me feel edgy,' he admitted.

'I'm sure Karl will soon get over his bad mood,' Jazz said cheerfully.

'He won't with Tracie Long egging him on,' Luke told her. 'She fancies Karl like mad. If he said the sky was green with red spots then as far as Tracie's concerned the sky would be green with red spots.'

Belle and Jazz turned their eyes heavenwards in mock despair. Younger than Tracie by quite a few years, neither of them were a jot interested in boys, other than ones like Luke who were their good friends. As for Karl Hogan with his huge, baggy clothes, big baseball boots and loud voice – forget it!

'I don't know why he turned so nasty all of a sudden,' Luke continued thoughtfully. 'I mean, we've been rehearsing for a few months now, getting on just fine. Having quite a laugh really. Then all of a sudden, wham, he's at me.'

'I'm sure it boils down to jealousy,' Belle said. Luke didn't look convinced.

'Maybe Karl's right,' he muttered. 'Maybe I *am* upstaging him.'

'Well, I think Helen's the one to put you straight

about that,' said Belle firmly. 'You shouldn't start changing your act just to please Karl, you know.'

'I will check it out with Helen,' Luke agreed.

'Why don't you ring her tonight instead of worrying about it all week?' Jazz urged.

It was a busy week, catching up on the homework they hadn't done at the weekend.

'Goodness,' yawned Jazz as she and Belle sat in the hot, stuffy library all through the lunch-hour. 'I wish I hadn't left this maths project to the last minute.'

Belle nodded her head as she frantically rubbed out a sum she'd done wrong three times.

'I'd rather be acting than doing this, any day!' she said wistfully. 'By the way, what happened with your parents? You never told me what they said about the drama club.'

Jazz beamed from ear to ear. 'They liked it a lot! Jamal told me that when they got home they were raving about Helen.'

'She's brilliant,' Belle agreed.

'They liked the kids too,' Jazz continued. 'Though they weren't so struck on some of the big boys.'

'Like Karl and Jerome?' Belle asked.

'Well, you've got to admit, they do look a bit heavy,' Jazz said.

'But appearances can be deceptive,' said Belle. 'I mean, look how nice Jerome was to Luke on Saturday.'

Jazz nodded. 'The only really nasty person seems to be Tracie Long. She didn't make them feel at all welcome.'

'She doesn't make anybody feel welcome,' Belle pointed out. 'Did your parents mention the Christmas show?'

'No, and I certainly won't!' Jazz replied.

'Careful,' Belle warned. 'No more lies.'

'It's all right for you,' Jazz exclaimed. 'You have no problems at home. Your parents don't mind what you do. I wish I was that lucky.'

'I know, I am lucky,' Belle agreed.

*　　　*　　　*

A few days later she changed her mind. After a grim parents' evening at school Mr and Mrs Forest came home livid.

'Your work's slipping and you're losing your concentration,' her dad reported back over breakfast the following morning. 'We're just not putting up with it, Belle,' he warned. 'This drama club business is a two-way deal. You do something for us and we'll do something for you. It's not an arrangement made entirely to suit you.'

Belle gazed at her cornflakes and felt tears prickling at the back of her eyes.

'I knew it would happen,' nagged Mrs Forest. 'Just as soon as you started that wretched drama club I knew you'd slip back to your old, silly ways.'

'They're not silly,' Belle remonstrated. 'I love acting!'

'Yes, we know that,' her mum replied wearily. 'But you can't afford to drop your education just because you want to be an actress.'

'Neither can you afford to take chances at the Charles Darwin school,' her dad continued. 'They expect a high standard all of the time. Let's face it, Belle,' said Mr Forest, rising from the table, 'it's academically much tougher than your old school and you're going to have to work a lot, lot, harder just to keep up.'

Belle sighed wearily. She didn't want to argue, it got her nowhere and put everybody in a bad mood for days. She'd told her parents umpteen times that she wanted to be an actress but they never, ever, took her seriously.

'You'll change your mind,' they always said. 'Just as soon as you grow up.'

Belle knew she would never change her mind but she had to be realistic. There were years and years to go until she was old enough to prove to her parents just how serious she was. Until then she had to keep the peace, work hard and not rock the boat. It was a fair compromise when she thought of what Jazz, Luke and Daisy had to put up with.

'So, Belle,' said her father as he was about to go, 'do we have an understanding about your priorities?'

She nodded. 'Yes,' she answered, looking him straight in the eye. 'Work first, play later.'

'Good girl,' he murmured, tousling her hair as he pecked her on the cheek.

As Belle helped Ben scoop up the last of his Coco-Pops she let out a long sigh of relief. Thank goodness she'd never told her parents she was understudying the main part in the *Oz* production. That would have really sent them over the edge!

CHAPTER NINE

★

Under Attack!

Saturday dawned bright and frosty. Belle and Jazz had arranged to meet at one o'clock in the theatre foyer. Both of them liked to get there early but they especially enjoyed the sophisticated theatre coffee bar! The prices were way out of their pocket-money range but they'd worked out that if they restricted themselves to a Coke with ice, lemon and two straws, and a chocolate doughnut or a blueberry Danish pastry they could just about afford it. Sitting on chrome chairs the girls slowly ate their treat, spinning it out for as long as they could.

'We'll meet up like this when we're rich and famous,' said Jazz, licking the rich chocolate sauce that squirted out of their shared doughnut. 'But then we'll have as many chocolate doughnuts as we want.'

'And blueberry pastries and freshly squeezed orange juice,' said Belle, joining in the fantasy.

'We'll scoff so much neither of us will be able to get into our costumes and that'll be the end of our brief but brilliant careers,' Jazz joked.

'Oh . . . do you really think we'll ever make it?' sighed Belle, leaning her head on her hand and staring dreamily into space.

'Who knows,' said Jazz, smiling at Belle's sky-blue eyes which had a faraway expression. 'Everybody you talk to – people like Helen who really knows the biz – they all say the same thing. It's not just a question of talent —'

'It's luck too,' said Belle, finishing the sentence for her.

'Something I don't have a lot of these days,' Jazz ended gloomily.

'Oh, come on, things *are* looking up,' Belle pointed out. 'At least you've not lied to your parents this Saturday, have you?'

'No, thank goodness! I told the truth, the whole truth and nothing but the truth. So help me!' said Jazz, holding her hand over her heart like she'd seen actors do in American courtroom dramas.

'I must say, my luck's run out at home,' Belle said. 'That blinking parents' evening really did for me.'

'We all seem to be under attack at the moment,' Jazz said. 'Still it's nice to know that other people are feeling just as hassled as I am.'

Belle quickly checked her watch.

'Where's Daisy?' she said. 'Didn't she say she'd get here a bit early for a natter?'

Jazz nodded. 'Maybe she got held up in the traffic. Her mum always drives her around in that big swanky Volvo.'

Belle drained the last dregs of Coke from their glass, then gulped. 'Oh-oh, don't look now. Here comes trouble.'

As she spoke Karl Hogan flung open the double doors and strode into the foyer. Seeing the girls he scowled and stomped into the hall. Before either of them could say a word Tracie Long swanned in, wearing tight black jeans that did nothing for her pencil-thin legs. Seeing the younger girls she flounced over, her big boots thumping heavily on the floor, and took up the argument exactly where she'd left off the week before.

'So you two are back,' she sneered. 'Hoping you'll get discovered and whisked off to Broadway, are you?'

'Stop picking on us,' Jazz blurted out angrily.

'Why shouldn't I?' Tracie demanded. 'You're friends of that pushy Luke Whelan, aren't you?'

'Yes!' both girls answered loyally.

'Then you'd better warn him that Karl's not putting up with any of his showing off this week.'

'For goodness sake, he's only playing his part,' Jazz cried.

'Oh, yeah? You'd know all about that, wouldn't you, Naomi Campbell?'

The argument could have turned really nasty but for Helen suddenly appearing in the foyer.

'Hello, girls,' she said, quickly taking in Tracie's belligerent expression. 'Everything all right?'

The younger two nodded; Tracie just shrugged her skinny shoulders.

'Good,' said Helen briskly. 'Shall we go in?'

Belle and Jazz scurried after her but Tracie slouched behind. The hall, as usual, was packed and loud with laughter. Belle quickly scanned the faces but there was still no sign of Daisy.

'Where is she?' Belle whispered to Jazz.

Helen solved the mystery after the warm-up exercises.

'Belle, can I have a word?' she said, quietly taking the girl on one side. 'Daisy's mum phoned me last night to say Daisy's got a touch of laryngitis. She won't be in today so you'll be understudying her sooner than you thought. Is that OK?'

Without a second's hesitation Belle instantly answered, 'Yes!' All her fears and self-doubts went right out of the window as her pulse raced with excitement and a wave of adrenaline zipped through her body.

'Good,' Helen beamed. 'You've got your copy of the script with you, haven't you?'

Belle nodded. It was safely tucked away in her rucksack.

'Have you had a chance to glance through it?' Helen inquired.

'Oh yes,' said Belle, not adding that the script had been her bedtime reading every single night for the last week and she knew Dorothy's part backwards, forwards and inside out!

'And I know you're pretty familiar with the songs,' Helen said with a smile, 'because I heard you singing most of them last week.'

Belle smiled and nodded eagerly.

'Right, group,' called Helen over the chatter. 'Daisy's sick, Belle's her understudy. Let's get this show on the road.'

Belle blushed to the roots of her pale hair as Tracie Long's mean eyes just about popped out of her head in blinding green envy.

'Star!' giggled Jazz, coming up from behind.

'Shh!' hissed Belle, starting to giggle too.

'Well, I suppose you've taken some of the heat off Luke,' Jazz added. 'Maybe Tracie will leave him alone this week.'

'Somehow I don't think so,' said Belle.

Throughout all the rehearsals Helen liked her students to wear part of their costumes. They never got to wear their complete costume until the dress-rehearsal but she liked them to have a little something that reminded them of their character. Luke, for example, had a straw hat and straw gloves. Karl always wore a hat rather like a tin pudding basin, and knee pads that forced him to walk jerkily. Jerome had a lion's mane and a long tail that regularly tripped somebody up. As the boys sorted out their props there was a bit of a scuffle and Belle saw Karl knock Luke off his feet as he bent down to pick up his straw hat.

'I meant what I said last week,' he hissed through clenched teeth. 'You muscle in on my scene one more time and I'll have you!'

Hearing the scuffle Helen turned from talking to Elvira and saw Luke sprawled all over the floor.

'What's all this?' she demanded.

'Nothing,' Karl replied, not looking at her.

'What's the problem, Luke?' said Helen, helping the boy to his feet.

'Nothing,' he answered, his face white with fear.

Suddenly, to everybody's complete surprise, Jerome said, 'There's a bit of aggro between these two and I'm getting really sick of it.'

'Thank you, Jerome,' said Helen. 'Would you like to expand, Karl?'

Karl scowled and looked as black as thunder.

'I don't like the way he –' he said, glaring at Luke, '– gets the biggest laughs during rehearsals.'

Said cold, in front of the group, it sounded really childish. One of the older boys snorted in disgust, which compelled Tracie to leap to Karl's defence.

'I've noticed Luke Whelan trying to outshine Karl,' she said with a flounce of her shoulders.

Helen took a deep breath and ignored Tracie, who was clearly spoiling for a fight.

'I think we'll talk about this in private,' she said to the three boys. 'Elvira, could you start the opening dance routine, please?'

Elvira nodded her head and started playing the music while everybody scrambled around for their dance shoes and music sheets.

Nobody knew what Helen said but ten minutes later

the three boys were back in the hall, looking a lot calmer.

'What happened?' Belle whispered to Luke as they waited in the wings.

'Can't tell you now,' he muttered back.

There wasn't a moment for Belle to ask another question. She was on, doing the tornado scene. Clutching the toy terrier that had superseded the rolled-up sweatshirt Belle skipped on stage.

'There's a tornado coming, Dorothy,' Aunty Em cried over the rising wind effects. 'A twister! Better run and hide in the cellar.'

Belle knew this was a tricky moment to co-ordinate. Dorothy has to run with Aunty Em towards the cellar while at the same time Toto jumps out of her arms and scampers off. Having carefully watched Daisy Belle knew she had to pretend to trip as she ran and throw the toy dog into the wings. Dorothy then goes off looking for Toto, and when she reappears on stage she trips over, bangs her head, loses consciousness and the dream of the land of Oz begins.

Belle adored every single second. A couple of times she missed her cue or got the wrong pitch for a song but she made it through the first hour with only a few wobbles.

'Well done, excellent,' called Helen. 'Take five.'

Belle was so buzzed up she could hardly sit down.

'Cool it,' laughed Jazz. 'Have a sip of orange juice and relax.'

'Thank you,' said Belle, taking the carton of juice and gulping thirstily.

'Leave some for me!' said Jazz, quickly retrieving her juice. 'You were good, Belle. Really excellent.'

Belle blushed at the unexpected praise.

'I was so busy trying to remember everything I didn't even notice what happened in Luke's scenes with Karl. Did it go OK?' she asked.

'No, they were terrible,' Jazz said. 'Luke was so self-conscious we hardly heard a word he was saying.'

'That's a shame,' said Belle, vividly remembering how brilliantly he had played his part in the previous weeks. 'What did Helen say?'

'Nothing much,' Jazz answered. 'The three of them were wooden. Lines all flat and automatic. I think Karl's really messed things up.'

Luke didn't join them for a natter as he usually did; he just sat alone, moodily staring into space.

The last hour whirled by but this time Belle paid particular attention to the boys' scenes and Jazz was right. They were terrible! Luke was lifeless, Jerome was cautious and Karl was way over the top.

'No, Karl!' Helen called out in sheer exasperation. 'Stop hamming it up. You've got to convince us that you're a bit soft under all that creaking tin, not Robocop! Think about it,' she said, looking Karl directly in the eyes.

'It's not a macho part,' Helen said. 'Try it softer.'

Karl tried it Helen's way and it worked.

'Well done, excellent,' she cried. 'You see how different that makes your character from Luke's. Scarecrow's a funny, dopey character. Brainless, stuffed with straw, he can hardly stand up straight. You're deeper, more thoughtful.'

Karl looked quite pleased by this definition and went into his character with fresh energy. Unfortunately Tracie Long sniggered at most of his attempts. After the third incident Helen lost her temper.

'Tracie, if I hear you laughing one more time you'll be out of this theatre and I won't have you back. Is that understood?'

Tracie looked surly but at least she shut up.

At five the group broke up and Helen congratulated

Belle on her performance. 'Well done,' she said warmly.

'It was such fun,' Belle enthused.

'Excuse me,' said Helen as she saw Luke sloping off. 'I need a word with this young man.'

She led Luke backstage and the minute she was out of hearing Tracie Long pounced.

'You were rubbish,' she snapped. 'The worst Dorothy I've seen so far.'

Belle tried to turn away and ignore her.

'And your singing. Ugh!' Tracie continued. 'Earache or what?'

Suddenly a deep voice boomed, 'Why don't you just put a sock in it, Tracie?'

Belle turned to gaze open-mouthed at Jerome.

'Why should I?' squeaked Tracie, clearly shaken.

'Because you're trouble,' Jerome said. 'You've messed up Luke, you tried messing up Karl and now you're all set to gut Belle. Leave it out, do you hear?'

Jerome eyeballed Tracie, who fled. Belle opened her mouth to thank Jerome but he disappeared as quickly as he'd appeared.

'He might be a person of few words but they certainly have the right kind of impact,' said Jazz. 'I've never seen Tracie Long shut up quite so quick before!'

CHAPTER TEN

★

Confidences

By Monday morning the girls were agog to find out what Helen had said to Luke after the rehearsal. Unfortunately they didn't manage to catch him alone all day Monday or Tuesday but on Wednesday lunchtime they found him without his ghastly brother.

'Hi,' said Belle. 'How's things?'

'Fine,' he answered cautiously.

Belle thought it best not to hassle him but Jazz blurted out, 'What happened with Helen?'

'She said I should try not to take things personally,' Luke answered.

'What?' Belle gasped. 'How could you possibly ignore Karl Hogan picking on you?'

'That's just what I said,' Luke replied. 'Helen explained that it's important in the biz to let things slide over you. If you take everything as a personal attack you'd be a nervous wreck.'

'But how do you ignore it?' Jazz puzzled. 'If somebody's mean to you it hurts and that feeling doesn't go away quickly.'

Belle instantly agreed. 'Even though I can't stand

blinking Tracie Long I still worry about all the horrible things she's said to me. I even dream about them, for goodness sake!'

'Helen's advice is, you've got to believe in yourself and not be pushed about by anybody.'

'She's right,' Belle agreed. 'But it must take a long time to learn how to do it.'

'That's why I'm starting right now,' Luke answered in a determined voice. 'Then by the time I get to drama school I'll be really sorted!'

'With a bit of luck there won't be any Karl Hogans at drama school,' Belle laughed.

'But there might be, so I'm working on it,' said Luke. 'Funny though, I reckon without Tracie Long winding us up Karl and I could be really good mates.'

'Tracie Long,' sniffed Jazz. 'She has an amazing talent for upsetting *everybody*!'

On Saturday Daisy was back, looking white and wan.

'Good to see you,' said Belle warmly. 'Is your throat any better?'

Daisy dropped her voice and whispered. 'It wasn't my throat, it was my dad.'

'Your dad! Did he ground you?' Belle asked.

'No, but he nearly found out,' Daisy explained. 'It

was a nightmare. Mum thought it safest for me to spend the afternoon at home, sweeping up leaves in the garden! I've never been so bored in my life.'

Helen swept in with Gilly the wardrobe mistress.

'Come along, kids,' she called. 'Costume fittings today.'

A ripple of excitement zipped along the Munchkin chorus line as Gilly measured them for their costumes. Their outfits were simple, cheap and very colourful. Red leggings, short yellow tops with a rainbow frill round the hem and enormous, floppy, sunflower hats that sent the entire cast into fits of laughter.

'Don't water that!' laughed Luke as Belle tried her hat on.

Gilly had hoped they wouldn't need shoes but the stage was a bit rough underfoot and a few of them had got splinters in their feet.

'Soft black ballet shoes will do or black slip-on plimsolls,' she suggested. 'Borrow some if you haven't got any.'

It was thrilling to see Gilly trying the different costumes on them all, taking in tucks or deftly adjusting hems, bodices and waists. When Luke, Jerome and Karl were fitted everybody stopped and stared in admiration. Even though the costumes were only half-finished the three of them looked stunning. Luke was covered in straw, from top to toe, with a robin's nest in one of his big, floppy pockets. Karl's costume had been sprayed to give it a silver metallic finish, and padded at the joints so that he could only move stiffly. Big, beefy Jerome looked uncharacteristically soft and cuddly in his bright yellow lion's outfit with its enormous fluffy mane and padded paws. Belle loved Dorothy's sweet blue and white gingham dress and little straw bonnet decorated with pale blue forget-me-not flowers. Best of all were the magic scarlet shoes covered in shimmering red sequins. The Wicked Witch of the East wore them to start with but Glinda, the Good Witch of the West, played by Rozzie, gave them to Dorothy. One of the most impressive costumes was that of the Wicked Witch of the East, but Tracie clearly hated it. Long and black, it trailed behind her like a dark snake. Her witch's hat was black and pointed and her nose was decorated with an enormous wart.

'The witch from hell!' giggled naughty Jazz.

'It's stupid!' yelled Tracie, as she yanked it off.

'Stop pulling it like that,' cried Gilly, red with anger. 'It's not even finished.'

103

'Huh!' snapped Tracie rudely.

'Somebody should have a word with you, madam!' seethed Gilly as she stooped to pick up the discarded costume.

Helen did. Ten minutes later she hauled Tracie backstage where, unbeknown to her, Belle and Jazz were quietly painting the Munchkin set.

'I am up to here with you,' Helen seethed. 'First you undermine Luke —'

'I did not!' whined Tracie.

'You did,' Helen retorted. 'I heard you!'

Tracie scowled and scuffed her feet. 'Somebody had to support Karl —' she started.

'Have you ever taken the trouble to read *The Wizard of Oz* from cover to cover?' Helen demanded.

'Well . . .' Tracie said, trying to avoid the question.

'No, I think is the answer,' Helen said. 'Writers go to a lot of trouble trying to create a balance between the main plot and the central characters. It's not easy. It's a craft, a skill. If everybody had the same number of lines and the same presentation the play would never lift off the ground.' Helen took a deep breath and added, 'I'd like you to apologise to Gilly. You behaved appallingly out there.'

'I am not wearing that naff costume,' raged Tracie.

'It's meant to enhance your witch's character, not prettify it,' Helen snapped. 'Acting's not always about playing the part of the beautiful princess, you know.'

'There's no way I'm having a wart on my nose!' Tracie said.

Belle and Jazz nearly collapsed with laughter when they heard this remark. Jazz made things ten times worse by dabbing a blob of black paint, which looked just like Tracie's wart, on the end of her nose.

'Just apologise to Gilly or you won't even be in the play,' Helen said as she turned on her heel and walked away.

'Phew!' gasped Belle when they'd gone. 'What a scorcher that was.'

'She really put Tracie straight,' Jazz replied.

'Somebody had to,' Belle said. 'With only three weekends to go before the dress-rehearsal we've all got to pull our weight!'

CHAPTER ELEVEN

★

Countdown!

December whooshed in, freezing cold and blowy. Cambridge was lit up for Christmas with strings of coloured lights all over the city centre. It was wonderful cycling over the bare, frosty common into Cambridge with its shop windows glittering bright, heaped up with festive toys and presents.

'Brrrr . . .' shivered Jazz as she and Belle changed into their leotards and leggings. 'I'll be glad when our costumes are finished. They might be a bit warmer than these skimpy things.'

'Then you'll be complaining you're too hot under the stage lights,' Belle teased.

'Oh, I'll have to get used to stage lights if I'm going to be a famous actress!' Jazz answered grandly.

Belle threw her ballet shoes at her. 'Bighead!' she joked.

'Come along, girls,' Helen called impatiently. 'We haven't a minute to lose.'

The pressure was on these days. There were no more leisurely long breaks or chats as they queued up by the drinks machine, or having a laugh with Rozzie

and Millie backstage. It was work . . . work . . . work –
and they loved it!

What with dodging wet sets, side-stepping Gilly's
growing mountain of costumes and avoiding Elvira's
sharp tongue, it was quite a stressful afternoon, but
working under pressure had its advantages. Suddenly
they were a team, supporting each other. They helped
each other shift sets, remember cues, find lost props,
even shared their lunches. If something went wrong
there was always an understanding laugh or a kind,
comforting word. It felt good, really good, as if they
were a big, happy family. Karl, Jerome and Luke had
really bonded since Helen had talked to them on the
subtle differences of their *Oz* characters. These days
they were more often to be found having a laugh than
a row.

'Come on, lads, get a grip,' Helen called as the
three of them shared a private joke. 'We've work to do
and I need your complete, undivided attention.'

The only fly in the ointment was Tracie Long who
still hated Belle and Luke and took every opportunity
to slip in a snide remark about either of them, so long
as Helen was out of hearing.

'You were rubbish this morning,' said Tracie to

Luke over break. 'Really messed things up. Didn't you think so, Karl?'

'No,' Karl answered coldly. 'I think he did just fine.'

Tracie's jaw dropped so far her chin nearly hit the floor!

'What did you think, Jerome?' asked Karl, turning to the older lad. 'Didn't Luke do OK?'

'Yeah,' Jerome replied in his usual laid-back way. 'The only problem was the Wicked Witch, she missed her cue every time.'

Tracie glared at the three boys who giggled at her furious face.

'That's it, Karl. We're history!' she shrieked as she flounced off into the ladies' toilets.

'Phew! That's a relief,' smiled Karl.

Daisy was in good spirits that Saturday.

'Everything all right?' Belle asked as they queued up together at the drinks machine. Daisy nodded and smiled.

'Dad's really busy these days, working all weekend, which is lousy for him but lucky for me.'

'That's good,' said Belle.

'Not quite,' Daisy added, dropping her voice to a whisper. 'He's talking of going skiing at Christmas.' Belle wrinkled her brow, puzzled.

'So what's the problem?'

'Only that we'd go in the middle of the show's run,' Daisy explained.

'No!' Belle gasped.

'Mum's determined not to go away for Christmas,' Daisy continued. 'She keeps saying she wants to spend Christmas at home with the family.'

'Thank goodness!' said Belle with genuine relief.

'Sometimes I wonder why I do this,' murmured Daisy.

'It won't always be this bad,' Belle assured her.

'No, it could get a lot worse!' Daisy joked.

Belle felt exhausted by the end of the week. She was working flat out at school preparing for the end of term exams which, no way, could she afford to do badly in. If she did *The Wizard of Oz* would be her first and only play with the Cambridge Drama Club.

'Are you all right?' asked her mum over breakfast on Saturday morning.

'Fine,' Belle answered cheerily. 'Just a bit sleepy,' she added, trying to stifle a yawn with the back of her hand.

'Well, be careful you don't go and get what Ben has,' Mrs Forest replied. 'He's been coughing all night and has a raging temperature. I shall have to get the doctor out. I'm sure it's flu.'

I mustn't get ill, thought Belle as she started on her Frosties. I must stay well until the play's over.

When she got to the drama club she discovered that half the cast were down with flu. Helen looked ghastly but it was nothing to do with the flu epidemic, she was worried sick.

'Daisy's not here,' she announced. 'Neither are half the Munchkins. Tracie's off too.' The sigh of delight that followed this particular piece of news even brought a smile to Helen's tired face. 'Is there anybody who could stand in for Tracie?' she asked.

'There's nobody in the world quite like Tracie!' Luke answered making everybody laugh.

'Come on, let's get real,' Helen said. 'I desperately need a Wicked Witch of the East today. I've got all her lighting cues to do with the stage manager and they're the most complicated of the lot.'

Jazz's hand slowly snaked up.

'I will,' she said, self-consciously.

'Excellent,' said Helen, with relief. 'So, for the moment, Jazz will play the Wicked Witch of the East. Belle will take Daisy's part. I'll have to play the Lion and Elvira will help out Rozzie and Millie in the depleted Munchkin line-up,' Helen finished.

It was the best and funniest rehearsal ever. Belle adored playing Dorothy and this time, without Tracie Long criticising her every move, she threw herself into the singing, giving it her all. Even Elvira applauded her 'Over the Rainbow' which was praise indeed.

'Wonderful, Belle,' she cried. 'Well done.'

As Belle left the stage she crossed with Jazz, dithering nervously in the wings.

'You'll be fine,' Belle whispered to her as Jazz adjusted her witch's hat. 'Just enjoy it. Have fun!'

Jazz did more than that. She whooshed on stage, cackling and shrieking with her black hair streaming out behind her like a dark cloud. Though she didn't know all the lines she nevertheless kept the pace going. What stunned everybody was her delivery, her presence on stage was electrifying.

'Wow!' gasped Rozzie and Millie, watching from the wings with Belle. 'She's brilliant.'

Belle nodded and smiled proudly. 'The best,' she murmured.

By the end of that Saturday class Belle and Jazz were as high as kites.

'I'm far too excited to even think of going home,' Jazz said.

'Me too,' Belle agreed as they plonked down on the plush sofas in the theatre foyer. 'Wasn't it a great day?'

Jazz nodded, her eyes huge and dreamy.

'When Helen asked for volunteers to play the Wicked Witch I was dying to put my hand up, but I hadn't the nerve. I was sure one of the older ones would jump at the chance.'

'But they didn't,' said Belle. 'And you were magic.'

'Helen's just asked me to be Tracie's official understudy,' Jazz added, breathless with delight.

'Yes!' cried Belle, jumping up and punching the air in excitement.

'It's excellent,' said Jazz with a big grin. 'But I bet you any money Tracie Long will be on the warpath next week.'

CHAPTER TWELVE

★

Like a Family

Tracie Long was back the following Saturday but Daisy wasn't.

'Where *is* she?' fretted Belle.

'Why don't you ring her and find out?' Jazz suggested.

'Great idea,' cried Belle. 'What if Mr Belham-Thomas should pick up the phone – what do I say? I'm Daisy's friend from drama club!'

'Of course not,' Jazz laughed. 'Surely you could bluff your way through? I'm serious Belle, Daisy might need a friend to talk to right now.'

Before Belle could answer Tracie Long thundered up, red in the face and out for trouble.

'You!' she snarled. 'How dare you snitch my part?'

Jazz stood rooted to the spot. She'd expected a bit of aggravation but not open violence like this.

'I was asked to play it,' she retorted. 'You were off sick, remember?'

'Creep!' Tracie ranted, her screeching voice echoing all round the hall. 'I'm sick of the pair of you. First it's her,' she said, stabbing a finger in Belle's direction, 'muscling in on the lead part, and then you, grabbing my part the minute my back's turned.'

'Hi, Trace,' called Karl, who'd been standing behind Tracie, listening to every word she'd said to Jazz. 'When did you get over the flu then?'

'Oooh, it was terrible!' Tracie answered dramatically. 'I was in bed all week. Even lost my voice,' she added self-pityingly.

'Lucky Jazz was able to step in like she did then,' Karl answered with a cheeky wink. 'I mean, it's difficult to be in two places at once, isn't it?'

Realising she'd been set up sent Tracie into an enormous rage.

'Humph!' she said as she stomped off across the room.

'Thanks, Karl,' said Jazz, gratefully.

'That's all right,' he answered evenly. 'Just let me know if you have any more trouble. I'm an expert on sorting out Tracie these days!'

Helen called the group together and handed round sheets of printed paper.

'OK, here's the running order,' she announced. 'As you can see next week's going to be a heck of a week! Let's go down the list together, then you can ask me questions if it's not clear.'

She waited until everybody had a copy of the schedule then started.

'Monday evening, six till nine, full run-through with all the cast, absolutely no excuses for not turning up promptly and ready for action. Tuesday, six till nine, we'll be doing the technical run for Act One. It'll be exhausting for everybody, but especially for Andy, the stage manager, who'll be on stage cueing the technical crew in the lighting box. We'll probably be working till the early hours so please bear with us if we get a bit shirty the following day!'

Older members of the group smiled knowingly.

'We remember what a state you were in last year,' they joked.

'Six till nine on Wednesday,' Helen continued. 'The tech run for Act Two. If we're running overtime, which we usually do on a tech run, then we may just skip the dialogue and go for a cue to cue.'

'What's a cue to cue?' asked Belle.

'Where we go from one scene change to another, with lighting and sound effects, but leave out the dialogue. It saves on time when we're really pushed,' Helen explained. 'Thursday is the full dress-rehearsal with make-up, hair and costume. There's a good chance some of you will be late home that night, so please warn your parents in advance. I don't want earache the night before we open, thank you very much. Friday night is our first night, be here by six o'clock at the latest. We have two shows on Saturday, three and seven-thirty; two again on Sunday and then we strike the set and put everything away.' Helen let out a long breath as she finished.

Belle's stomach flipped right over in excitement and her pulse started to race. Words like technical run, full run-through, dress-rehearsal and opening night were the sweetest music in her ears. The bit she didn't like the sound of was the striking of the set when the show was over; it would be like putting away a bright golden dream.

'I warn you all, you'll be tired in the week and there'll be a few bust-ups, believe me,' Helen said, speaking from vast experience. 'But by opening night, when the adrenaline kicks in, you'll be as high as kites!' she promised.

Jazz squeezed Belle's arm. 'I just can't wait!' she hissed.

As the group broke up Helen drew Belle aside for a quiet word.

'Daisy's got the flu badly and she won't be in today or most of next week.'

'Is she *just* sick?' Belle asked, determined to know the truth.

Helen looked at her concerned face and nodded.

'Yes. I didn't realise Daisy had filled you in on her family troubles,' she said quietly.

'She did when I started to understudy her part,' Belle explained. 'The last time we talked she was worried about her dad taking them off on a skiing holiday for Christmas.'

'Yes, Mrs Belham-Thomas warned me of that,' Helen said grimly. 'But she's determined the family will spend Christmas here in Cambridge. I only hope her plan works out,' said Helen, holding up two crossed fingers. 'Anyway, judging from the weather reports there's no snow. Maybe that'll put that wretched man off,' she muttered under her breath.

'Do you think Daisy will make the dress-rehearsal on Thursday?' Belle asked.

'Who knows,' Helen replied.

Poor, poor Daisy, thought Belle. Her life was so stressful, no wonder she was ill. Blow Mr Belham-Thomas, she thought. Come what may, I'm jolly well going to phone Daisy tonight.

That night, as soon as she got home, Belle did

phone Daisy and her worst fears were realised. Mr Belham-Thomas answered.

'Hello, Charles Belham-Thomas speaking.'

Belle gulped then put on her poshest voice.

'Hello. I'm Isabella. May I speak to Daisy?' she asked with cloying politeness.

'Hold on, I'll get her,' came back his answer.

Belle waited tensely, her heart thumping loudly against her ribs. When Daisy picked up the phone she let out a long sigh of relief.

'Hi,' she said. 'It's Belle.'

Daisy giggled. 'I wondered who on earth Isabella could be,' she said, her voice sounding hoarse and sore. 'How are you?'

'Never mind me!' Belle replied. 'How are you? Jazz and I are worried sick about you.'

'I'm really weak,' Daisy answered. 'This wretched flu's just wiped me out.'

'But you must get well, and soon,' Belle said staunchly. 'We're missing you.'

'How's it going?' Daisy asked, dropping her voice to a cautious whisper. 'Are you all right?'

'Fine, it's fun,' Belle answered honestly. 'Unfortunately I'll never sing like you. There are some bits of "Over the Rainbow" when I know I sound like a love-sick frog!'

Daisy giggled again.

'Oh, Belle. You're really cheering me up.'

'It's good to know my voice can cheer somebody up,' Belle joked.

'Come on, tell me all the gossip,' Daisy urged.

'Well, Jazz understudied for Tracie when she was off sick and Tracie went ape.'

'Stupid girl!' cried Daisy, scandalised.

'Jerome, Karl and Luke are getting on just fine and Elvira's colour schemes have moved into purple and silver.'

Daisy laughed so much it brought on a coughing spasm.

'Oh, drat. Here comes Dad,' she spluttered. 'I've got to go.'

'No, no,' Belle cried. 'Wait. When will you be able to come back?'

'I'm hoping I'll be well enough for the dress-rehearsal, at least,' came back her muffled reply, then the line went dead.

When Belle showed her parents the schedule for the following week they both looked quite worried. When she told them she'd be understudying the lead part they got very hot and bothered.

'It's so much work, Belle,' cried her mother. 'And you'll be out every night,' she added as her eyes scanned Helen's information sheet.

'Understudying the lead role is an enormous responsibility,' Mr Forest grumbled.

'It's only for the rehearsals,' Belle said quickly.

'How do you know?' her dad asked sharply. 'Daisy might be ill all next weekend too.'

'And you've got your exams at the beginning of the following week,' Mrs Forest pointed out.

'Then we break up for the Christmas holidays,' Belle said, determined to introduce a lighter note into the conversation.

'Heck!' her dad exclaimed. 'You've taken on a lot, that's for sure.'

Belle tried to hide her own anxieties by smiling brightly.

'I've been doing lots of revision recently,' she said with a confidence she certainly didn't feel.

Mr Forest gave her a look she knew too well. It meant, don't try and hoodwink me, young lady.

The following week was the strangest mixture of

wonderfully exciting and incredibly exhausting. Knowing there would be no chance of doing a stroke of work in the evenings, Jazz and Belle worked all through their lunch-hours in the school library. On Monday, to their complete amazement, Luke joined them.

'Goodness,' Belle said. 'Is your mum pushing you to do well in the exams too?'

'No, it's cold out there and warm in here,' Luke said, as usual turning a serious issue into a joke.

Both girls exchanged a smile. They guessed that Luke was working hard just to please his mum. Jazz chewed the end of her pencil as Luke opened his maths book.

'Have you thought how you're going to get out of the house for the next seven nights without upsetting your brothers?' she asked him.

'I'll be ducking and diving,' Luke answered with a crafty wink. 'Nipping out to the youth club, popping round to see a friend, meeting Mum from bingo. Stuff like that,' he explained. 'What about you?' he asked.

Belle held her breath. This was the question that had been burning her lips for weeks but she'd never dared ask it.

'I'm going to tell them the truth, sort of,' Jazz

answered. 'Like I'm working every night on the show, which is the truth – isn't it?'

Luke and Belle nodded.

'But what if they want to come and see it?' Belle insisted.

'I'll tell them the tickets have sold out,' Jazz retorted.

'Maybe they'll come anyway,' Luke suggested.

'Then they'll get the shock of their lives and I'll be out of the drama club,' Jazz answered flatly. 'I'm not going to start lying again.'

'I wouldn't either,' Belle agreed. 'Your parents are really sweet.'

'I know,' Jazz replied. 'Sometimes I wish they were horrible, then I wouldn't feel quite so guilty as I do.'

'If they were horrible like my brothers you wouldn't even care,' Luke assured her.

The three friends stared at each other and smiled.

'It's funny how we've got to know each other,' Belle said.

'It's the drama club, it has that effect on people,' Luke replied. 'It makes you sort of stick together.'

'Like a family,' Jazz said with a smile.

'A really good family,' Luke added.

CHAPTER THIRTEEN

★

Dress Rehearsal

Tuesday evening was a nightmare. It was their first technical run and Andy, the stage-manager, looked as if he was on the edge of a nervous breakdown! He was backstage cueing the technicians in the lighting box at the back of the theatre, while Helen ran back and forth between them, getting more frantic with every passing hour. To Belle and Jazz it all seemed immensely complicated, in fact half the time they hadn't a clue what was going on. All they knew was that each scene had a lighting change and usually sound effects, and that these two things had to happen at exactly the right moment otherwise it looked ridiculous. There was no point in Dorothy saying, 'Ah! Here comes the twister!' and whirling offstage, apparently caught up in a tornado, if the stage stayed brightly lit like a hot summer's day. Sound effects for the storm had to happen during the storm, not ten minutes afterwards!

Sometimes it was tedious for the cast, who had to hold positions or repeat an entry over and over again just to get the lighting absolutely right with the scene change. Most of Dorothy's scenes were technically pretty complicated but Belle enjoyed all of them, apart from one tense moment when she had a quick costume change, between the tornado and the scene where she arrived in the Land of Oz. Her plain dress had to be swopped for the blue and white gingham dress which Gilly had made specifically for her once she started understudying Daisy. Belle dashed into the wings, grabbed the dress and scrambled into it.

'I'm stuck!' she squeaked.

Rozzie and Millie tugged on either side of the dress but it was stuck across Belle's chest. With her arms poking out and the dress only half covering her Belle looked ridiculous! Rozzie and Millie, characteristically, started to laugh their heads off as Belle struggled, unable to get the wretched dress either on or off!

'What is going on?' snapped Helen as Belle missed her cue.

'I'm stuck!' wailed Belle, tottering out from the wings. Stressed as she was even Helen smiled.

'Gilly,' she called. 'What's happened here?'

Gilly took one look at the dress and laughed.

'That's Daisy's dress!' she said. 'I must've put the

wrong one out. I'm sorry, Belle. Let me help you out of that before you suffocate.'

Many hilarious mistakes happened that evening. People lost their props, their costumes and their lines! At least half of them had a moment or two of unexpected nerves and just dried up on stage. Even Luke, normally so cool and on top of things, lost his place twice. Jerome lost his temper when Tracie tripped over his tail and pulled it off, and the boy who was playing the Wizard of Oz nearly choked when Andy went mad with the smoke machine!

By nine o'clock the entire cast were hot and exhausted.

'OK,' Helen called. 'Off you go. Get a good night's sleep, see you back here tomorrow, six o'clock sharp, when I hope most of our technical difficulties will be sorted out.'

Luke, Belle and Jazz stopped at the chip shop in the shopping precinct and bought a bag of fish and chips each which they ate as they waited for Belle's dad to pick them up in the car. The fish was hot and crispy, just what they needed as they huddled together against the icy-cold wind that was blowing around the brightly lit streets.

'I bet Helen and Andy will be working till two or

three in the morning,' Luke said as he hungrily nibbled his chips.

'The things they do for us,' said Jazz gratefully.

'We should have bought them a bag of chips,' Belle said, hungrily polishing off all the scrappy bits soaked in vinegar at the bottom of her bag.

'Too late,' said Luke, throwing his rubbish into the nearby litter bin. 'Here comes your dad.'

Belle didn't realise just how tired she was until she slumped into the warm seat beside her dad.

'Good rehearsal?' Mr Forest asked cheerfully.

'Great,' she answered, smothering a yawn. Even Luke's lively chatter faded as they cruised through the empty streets. Mr Forest dropped each off in turn then headed home with Belle.

'Are you all right, love?' he said anxiously.

Belle nodded and smiled blissfully.

'Oh, dad,' she sighed. 'It's wonderful!'

Wednesday evening was the technical run for Act Two. It was better and faster than the previous evening because Helen and Andy had worked out most of the technical problems. In fact it was all going rather too slickly. Instead of holding their positions, as they had done the previous night, the cast weren't quick enough and kept on missing their lighting cues.

'Come on, come on,' cried Helen, who had enormous dark circles under her eyes. 'You're supposed to be in position in the spotlight, Belle, not running into it. Do it again.'

'Sorry,' Belle called from the back of the stage. 'I couldn't see the marker in the dark.'

'Of course you can't see it,' Helen snapped. 'You have to remember it!'

Seeing Belle's crestfallen face Helen smiled and said, 'I did warn you that we might be a bit frayed round the edges by this point in the rehearsals. Andy and I were working here till nearly dawn, so we're a bit frazzled. OK?'

Belle nodded. 'OK,' she answered.

'So,' said Helen briskly, 'when the lights fade down, creep across the stage on to your mark and the spot will come on you as Elvira plays the opening chords for "Over the Rainbow". I want you in that spotlight, looking lost and bewildered, and bringing a lump to every throat in the house.'

Belle nodded. She wouldn't have a problem looking lost and bewildered – she was utterly lost and bewildered! Luckily her second attempt went better than the first.

'Excellent, we're getting there,' said Helen. 'But Belle, I want real pathos when you're doing "Over the Rainbow". There shouldn't be a dry eye in the house.'

Belle nodded.

'I'll do my best,' she promised, but she knew she could never sing like Daisy. Her voice was strong but average, Daisy was gifted and could wring the heart with her lilting, sweet melodies.

Thursday was the full dress-rehearsal, complete with costume, make-up and hair. The cast were completely wired up. Excitement had replaced fatigue and they were all at a high pitch of nervous anticipation which sharpened everything they did. The first half went brilliantly, even though Andy did his usual trick and nearly choked the entire cast with the smoke machine!

Back-stage poor Gilly was going mad! Buttons popped off, seams split, wigs slipped, make-up melted and tempers snapped left, right and centre. Predictably, Tracie Long's was the first to snap! Her wig was too hot, her hat was too big and the red magic shoes were killing her! With seventeen others to dress Gilly hadn't time to pamper to Tracie's every whim.

'You'll just have to put up with it,' she said briskly as she attended to Jerome's mane, which kept coming unravelled.

'I jolly well won't,' squawked Tracie. 'You've got to do something about this stupid wig right now!'

Gilly looked as if she would explode with fury. Luckily Jerome came to her aid.

'Tracie, if you don't shut up,' he said very quietly but with definite menace in his voice, 'I'll strangle you with my tail.' His dark threat instantly silenced Tracie but reduced Gilly to hysterics. She laughed so much she had to sit down.

In the second act poor Luke dried up. 'Er ... er ...' he dithered, his mind a blank.

Helen prompted him by saying the first few words and Luke immediately remembered the rest. Five minutes later exactly the same thing happened to Belle, then Jerome, then Rozzie who giggled helplessly.

'It's just nerves,' Helen reassured them. 'You know your lines, all of you. For goodness sake, you've been learning them long enough. If it happens on the night don't panic. Andy will prompt you and you simply carry on as if nothing had ever happened.'

The rehearsal ran way over time, it was a hundred minutes instead of the scheduled ninety.

'But we've never done it with make-up and hair before,' flapped Rozzie. 'They take so long to get right,' she added, irritably straightening Glinda's golden wig which kept slipping sideways over her ears.

'Don't worry,' Helen soothed. 'That's what rehearsals are about, bringing everything perfectly together.'

'Perfect be blowed!' muttered Jazz whose Munchkin tunic had split down the back the minute she'd set foot on stage.

'Everything will be fine on the night,' Helen promised with a confidence they certainly didn't feel. 'There's nothing like a live audience to keep you on your toes.'

The words 'live audience' made Belle's stomach plummet. She knew the Library Theatre sat four hundred, but how many would turn up for the first night? Helen answered the question for her.

'I've checked with the box-office bookings,' she said, 'and there are over a hundred seats sold. We usually have huge sales on the door so it should be a respectable audience. About two or three hundred I'd guess.'

Belle knew that a lot of the cast members' families and friends were coming to the opening night but she'd begged her parents not to.

'I'll be a bag of nerves,' she explained. 'Come on the final night when I'm really in the swing.'

After the final rehearsal the mood was high and tense in the girls' dressing-room. There were costumes everywhere. Make-up lay littered across every available surface, wigs and hats dangled from chairs, hooks, mirrors and doorknobs.

'Put your costumes back on your hangers, which are all named,' Gilly shrieked over the din. 'Return them to me for a final check. If your costume gets lost it's *your* problem,' she added. 'Not mine!'

Worried sick that she was going to smear make-up over Dorothy's gingham dress, Belle gingerly stepped out of it, carefully put it on the hanger, and carried it over to Gilly who added it to the costumes in her wardrobe.

'I'm a Munchkin costume short,' Gilly yelled as she counted the tunic-tops.

'Mine,' Jazz shouted as she wove her way through the sea of bodies and handed in her outfit.

'Ah!' said Gilly, reaching for her needle and cotton. 'Your's is the one that split halfway through the performance. You've not put on weight, have you?' she asked as she gave Jazz the once-over.

'Me!' gasped Jazz, as slim as a reed in her vest and leggings. 'If only I could.'

'Well you might have to wear Belle's tomorrow if I don't get this finished in time,' Gilly added frantically.

Belle stopped and stared at her Munchkin costume which she'd almost forgotten about. She'd played the part of Dorothy for so long now she'd forgotten how to be a Munchkin.

'Come on,' said Jazz, pulling her towards the dressing-table. 'Let's grab a seat and get this greasy make-up off.'

They sat, squashed up together on a single stool, at the long bench-like dressing-table which all the girls shared. A mirror surrounded by bright lights ran the length of the dressing-table, showing every spot and blemish on their faces.

'Can I borrow your cleanser?' Jazz asked. 'Mine won't shift this rouge.'

Belle dived into her rucksack, stuffed full of cotton wool balls and creams, and brought out her cleanser.

'Help yourself,' she said.

Jazz busily applied the cream to her red cheeks,

then stopped to laugh at Belle staring into the mirror, her face soft and dreamy.

'Oh, wasn't it good?' Belle sighed ecstatically.

Before Jazz could answer there was a mocking laugh from the other end of the dressing-table.

'Check out the poser!' yelled Tracie Long.

Belle jumped self-consciously and turned quickly away from the mirror.

'Getting used to playing the star, are you?' sneered Tracie. 'Well, I wouldn't be too sure of yourself, Belle Forest. If Daisy doesn't turn up tomorrow the show will take a serious nosedive. A flop, I'd say, with amateurs like you hamming it up.'

Belle tried desperately hard to hold back the tears that threatened to spill out of her eyes and humiliate her right there in front of the despicable Tracie Long. Suddenly Rozzie, Millie and Jazz were surrounding her, like bodyguards.

'Leave her alone,' stormed Millie.

'You're just jealous because Belle's done a brilliant job,' snapped Rozzie.

To Belle's utter amazement all the girls in the dressing-room suddenly took her side.

'Yes, leave her alone.'

'Belle's done all right.'

'None of us could have done any better,' they chorused.

This time the tears that threatened to flow from Belle's eyes were those of gratitude.

'Thank you, thank you,' she gulped.

'Humph!' said Tracie Long. Deflated as a popped balloon she walked into the ladies' toilets to remove her make-up.

'Good riddance,' said Jazz.

'That's shown her,' laughed Millie.

'Perhaps she'll leave you in peace from now on,' said Rozzie.

Belle shook her head. 'I've got an awful feeling that Tracie Long won't leave me in peace until Daisy comes back.'

CHAPTER FOURTEEN

★

First Night Nerves

The next day, Friday, Belle could hardly concentrate on anything. Would she be understudying – or not? Should she phone Daisy and find out for sure whether she'd be coming? In the playground she anxiously poured out her anxieties.

'Stay calm,' Jazz advised.

'I *can't*!' Belle shrieked. 'The suspense is killing me. I don't know whether I'm a Munchkin or Dorothy and the uncertainty is driving me round the bend. Do you think I should phone Daisy and find out one way or the other?' she demanded.

Jazz thought hard for a few minutes, clearly finding it difficult to make her mind up.

'No, I don't think so,' she finally said. 'If she's worse she's bound to be in bed and there's a good chance she won't answer the phone anyway. You wouldn't want to speak to her dad again.'

'That's just what I thought,' Belle agreed. 'I'll just have to sweat it out,' she finished grumpily, but the long, boring hours at school dragged by at a snail's pace. By five Belle was so tense she simply couldn't eat.

'Come on, Belle, you must have something,' insisted her mum. 'You'll feel sick on an empty stomach.'

'I'll feel sick on a full one,' Belle replied. 'Perhaps I'll just have a cup of tea and a slice of toast,' she said, hoping to appease her mother.

'How about beans on toast?' Mrs Forest fussed.

'No, Mum,' Belle answered. 'Just something plain, the plainer the better. Don't worry, I'll make it myself.'

The food, followed by a long soak in a hot bath, helped her nervous butterflies, then it was time to leave. It was a wet, windy night so Belle was particularly grateful to her dad for driving her to the Library Theatre. Along the way they picked up Luke and Jazz. When Mr Forest saw Mr and Mrs Khan on their doorstep waiting with Jazz, he wound down the car window and waved.

'See you at the theatre,' he called through the rain.

'Shh!' hissed Belle, giving him a warning poke in the ribs.

'Shh what?' Mr Forest asked, turning to her in astonishment. 'Don't they know about the show?'

'Yes, but they don't know Jazz is *in* it – on stage,' she explained.

'Oh! Do they think she's backstage?' he asked, completely puzzled.

Belle nodded. 'That's why she doesn't want them to come. Shh!' she said again, bringing the conversation to an abrupt end as Jazz climbed into the car.

They got to the theatre with time to spare.

'Thanks, Dad,' Belle called as they all jumped out. 'Wish me luck.'

'Lots of it, love,' he answered warmly. 'I only wish I could come along and see the opening night.'

'No way, not tonight,' Belle answered firmly.

The three children dashed up the four flights of stairs, giggling with nervous excitement. When they ran into the theatre foyer the first person Belle saw was Daisy! Her heart went up and then instantly went down. Her first reaction of delight was immediately replaced by one of bitter disappointment. After all the work, all the effort, all the anxiety she wasn't in fact going to play the lead role. It was back to the chorus line for Belle.

Without a moment's hesitation Daisy headed straight for her.

'I'm a lot better,' she said, her pretty face full of concern. 'Do you mind?'

Belle didn't quite know what to say so she shook her head, then nodded it!

'We've all missed you,' she answered honestly.

Mrs Belham-Thomas hurried up, an older version of Daisy with long auburn hair and the same gentle smile.

'Helen's just been telling me what a wonderful job you've done in Daisy's absence,' she said. 'I can't thank you enough. Daisy would have been fretting non-stop without you as her understudy.'

It was all getting a bit awkward for Belle who was feeling very confused. Fortunately Helen whooshed up, grabbed Daisy and said, 'Sorry, but I need you urgently. Bye, Mrs Belham-Thomas. Enjoy the show.'

Belle dashed into the girls' dressing-room desperately trying to remember her Munchkin lines.

'I can't even recall what a Munchkin sounds like,' she said to Jazz, desperately.

'Small and very squeaky,' Jazz reminded her. 'Like this . . .' Striking a funny pose Jazz crouched into a fat, dumpy shape and started to sing in a high-pitched voice, ' "We're off to see the wizard, the wonderful wizard of Oz".'

Laughing, Belle slipped into her costume and started to remember what a Munchkin felt like. When she joined the rest of the chorus line Rozzie and Millie were overjoyed to see her back. Giggling and very over-excited they peeped through a slit in the curtain after doing their warm-up exercises.

'Can you see my mum and dad?' Millie asked, standing on tip-toe to peer over Jazz's shoulder.

'Yes, they're right on the front row,' Jazz answered. 'Oh, I can see Luke's mum too. He'll be pleased.'

The note of longing in Jazz's voice made Belle's heart ache. In the semi-darkness she put her arm about her friend's shoulder and gave it a squeeze.

'It would be nice if one day my parents were out there,' Jazz murmured wistfully.

As the theatre filled up and the excited buzz from the auditorium grew louder and more expectant Elvira took her seat at the grand piano and started to play the theme music from the show. All the Munchkins hummed it quietly as they waited starstruck, in the wings! Andy, the stage-manager, white with nerves, called 'stand by' and the house lights dimmed. As Elvira's music faded away, the velvet stage curtain lifted with a gentle swoop and the Cambridge Children's Drama Club's production of *The Wizard of Oz* opened!

As Daisy did her first scene Belle whispered every word with her.

'Sit back and enjoy it,' Jazz suggested. 'It's not your responsibility any more.'

'I can't,' Belle explained. 'I'm on automatic pilot.'

'When we go out dancing you'd better remember you're a Munchkin,' Rozzie whispered.

'How could I forget with this sunflower on my head!' Belle giggled.

Because she'd missed the technical run rehearsals Daisy was having problems getting into the right spot at the right moment. Luckily the lighting technician was being extra cautious with the scene changes so Daisy did have a little time to get it right. One thing which was flawless, even after two weeks' illness, was Daisy's singing. Her looks, charm, grace and perfect voice brought the house down. After 'Over the Rainbow' there wasn't, as Helen had predicted, a dry eye in the house!

At the interval they all dashed back to the dressing-room to cool off, grab a drink and nip to the loos.

'Good to see Daisy back,' Tracie Long said in an over-loud voice as they queued for the toilets. 'I get sick of working with amateurs, don't you, Sharon?'

Sharon, her friend, who played Aunty Em, went red with embarrassment. She didn't answer Tracie's question but smiled apologetically at Belle, as if to say, She's nothing to do with me, really! Belle shrugged. As far as she was concerned the biggest perk about being back in the Munchkin line-up was getting Tracie Long off her back.

The audience took a long time to get back to their seats and even then their excited chatter hummed around the auditorium.

'They're really enjoying themselves,' said Jazz. 'You can just feel it in the air, like an electric current.'

She was right. The air was vibrant and it affected the entire cast. Everybody performed two hundred percent in that second half and Luke brought the house down with his hilarious Scarecrow. As Belle stood, drenched in the limelight, flanked by Jazz and Millie, she watched Luke, fascinated. He was a born actor and had the audience in his hands, making them laugh at his jokes and cry at his pathos.

But it was Daisy who stole their hearts away.

'She could melt stone with a voice like that,' Jazz whispered as the lights went down on Dorothy.

As the show romped to its finale the music got

louder and the singing more jubilant. When the cast came on to take their curtain call Belle really thought that the auditorium would cave in. The cheering, clapping, whistling and applauding just wouldn't stop. They took four curtain calls and then went into an encore of 'Follow the Yellow Brick Road'. Daisy was awash with flowers, so were Helen and Elvira. When the cast finally staggered off stage, exhausted but blissfully happy, they found a huge tin of Roses chocolates in their dressing-rooms and cans of chilled Coke.

'Fabulous,' sighed Belle, as she leaned her hot cheek on the cold Coke tin.

'Fabulous,' Jazz agreed as she chomped hungrily on a dark chocolate caramel.

Because of the curtain calls and encore, plus all the flowers and congratulatory hugs and kisses, it was nearly eleven o'clock by the time they got out of the theatre.

'Oh, isn't this the life, Belle?' Jazz cried. 'A weekend of heaven.'

'Four more wonderful performances,' sighed Belle dreamily.

'Then it's back to school for the rotten exams,' Jazz reminded her.

'I'm not even going to think of *that*,' answered Belle grandly.

'Agreed,' laughed Jazz. 'Here's to now and the merry, merry land of Oz!'

CHAPTER FIFTEEN

★

In The Limelight

For all her exhaustion Belle had a fitful night's sleep, full of bizarre dreams. It was a relief when morning came and she could get up and have breakfast downstairs with the family who were agog for all the news.

'Daisy came back,' she announced before they all asked too many awkward questions.

'Oh. . .' there was a noticeable sigh of disappointment around the table.

'That must've been tough for you, love,' said her dad thoughtfully. Belle nodded.

'It was to start with but I had such fun with all my friends in the chorus line I actually forgot all about it.'

'Well, I'll be disappointed not to see you in the lead part on the final night,' said Chris. 'I was looking forward to that.'

'We'll enjoy the show whatever part Belle plays,' Mrs Forest added warmly.

*　　　　*　　　　*

There wasn't time to come home in between the two Saturday performances so Belle and Jazz took a packed tea and ate it with all their friends in the

144

Library Theatre foyer. They'd been given enough money by their parents for a hot drink so they sat in total luxury, sipping frothy hot chocolate as they shared out their assorted food. Daisy had her dainty sandwiches of ham, cheese and cucumber, Rozzie and Millie had sausage rolls and crisps, and Jazz had brought along a bagful of the best vegetable samosas they'd ever tasted in their lives.

'Mmm,' drooled Belle as she bit into the crisp flaky pastry.

'My mum made them,' said Jazz proudly. 'Look, she's sent half a dozen for Helen.'

Belle had some home-made Cornish pasties and some delicious chocolate fudge cake and Luke had nothing at all.

'I was in such a hurry to get out I forgot,' he admitted.

The girls had more than enough and instantly heaped loads of goodies on to a paper plate for Luke.

'Did your mum enjoy it last night?' Jazz asked.

'Loved it,' said Luke through a mouthful of pastie. 'She said I reminded her so much of my dad it made her cry.'

'If your mum liked it maybe your brothers would like it too,' Belle said thoughtfully.

'No way!' Luke answered. 'But my mum's coming again tonight and tomorrow,' he added proudly. Seeing Jazz's sad expression he said, 'How about you, Jazz. How's it going?'

'My mum and dad were pretty narked I was so late home every night last week,' she answered.

'Have they asked to come and see the show?' Luke said.

'No, and I've not mentioned it either,' Jazz told him flatly.

Belle didn't say anything but she could tell from the look in Jazz's topaz yellow eyes that she would have loved her parents to come along to the show – and enjoy it.

The Saturday night audience were wonderful. They laughed at all the jokes, joined in the songs and simply wouldn't let the cast off stage, even after four curtain calls.

'We're going to be here all night,' cried Belle, breathless with excitement.

'We'll do an encore, then we'll bring the curtain down and leave it down,' Helen instructed Andy.

The encore of 'Over the Rainbow' brought the audience to their feet but finally they let the cast go and the applause fizzled from a thunderous crescendo to a smattering of claps and a few whistles.

Helen had a few things to discuss with the main actors, 'giving notes' she called it, but the chorus line were allowed to go home.

'You're all exhausted,' said Helen, smiling at the row of sleepy Munchkins. 'After today I promise you tomorrow will be a breeze.'

She couldn't have said anything that was further from the truth!

On Sunday the gang of four, Belle, Jazz, Millie and Rozzie, arrived at the theatre earlier than anybody else, as usual, for no good reason other than all of them had one thing in common – they just loved spending the whole day there, together! The twins' mum had sent a chocolate cake for the cast which they were planning to hand round at teatime. Rozzie had brought a pack of cards, Jazz had her Gameboy, but they finished up spending the whole day chatting or playing hide and seek backstage.

At two-thirty Helen came into the girls' dressing-room, looking white and tense.

'Belle,' she called over the racket.

Belle didn't need to be told anything. The minute she saw Helen's face she knew.

'It's Daisy,' Helen said, as she drew her into a quiet corner. 'Her wretched father announced that they were having lunch with an important colleague of his who lives in Suffolk.'

She paused, clearly livid. 'Thank goodness Mrs Belham-Thomas got a minute to phone me. She's distraught.'

'I don't believe it!' Belle spluttered. 'You'd think they could have made *some* excuse.'

'I'm sure they tried but I get the impression they're all scared to death of him,' said Helen. 'Come along, now,' she said, glancing at her watch. 'We've only thirty minutes to curtain up. Change as quickly as you can then I'll get Elvira to do some voice exercises with you.'

Belle dashed into the dressing-room, grabbed her Dorothy dress from the rail and hastily put it on.

'Is Daisy sick again?' asked Jazz.

'No,' Belle gasped as she turned round for Jazz to do up her zip. 'Mr Belham-Thomas has taken them all off to Suffolk for lunch! Can you believe it?'

Jazz was incredulous, so were Rozzie and Millie who

hurried over to Belle when they saw her changing into Dorothy's pretty gingham dress.

'Sure you're not wearing Daisy's costume?' teased Millie.

'Absolutely,' Belle answered as she twirled round. 'Now where are my shoes and socks? Gilly said she was going to leave them in a box with my name on it.'

'Here,' said Rozzie, crawling underneath the costume rail. The happy, friendly atmosphere was shattered by the appearance of Tracie Long. She stopped dead in her tracks when she saw Belle dressed for the main part.

'Not amateurs again,' she sneered.

This time Belle really lost her temper.

'OK, Tracie,' she snapped. 'You play Dorothy's part. Here, help me get out of this dress and you take over.'

Tracie's face dropped. Belle had clearly called her bluff and she hadn't a clue what to say.

'Well, come on,' urged Belle. 'You're capable of playing the lead part, do it. We haven't got all day.'

Tracie Long's thin face went as black as thunder before she turned on her heel and walked off.

'Well done!' cried Millie.

'That shut her up,' added Rozzie with glee.

'Sorry, got to go,' gasped Belle as she saw the minute hand ticking slowly towards three.

Elvira had ten minutes to give Belle a few voice warm-up exercises, then the audience started filing into the auditorium. Belle's stomach churned. She'd never expected to play Dorothy for real – now it was happening. Would she make it?

Seeing her nervous face Helen said, 'Go backstage and take a few deep breaths in peace and quiet.'

Millie, Rozzie and Jazz saw Belle slip away and understood the reason why.

'Better leave her alone,' said Jazz.

At three o'clock the auditorium fell quiet as Elvira played the opening music. When the velvet stage curtain swung up, revealing a sea of faces, Belle gulped and then adrenaline took over. It was a wonderful, wonderful show and the greatest thing about it was the support she got from the rest of the cast. When she stumbled over the opening line of 'Over the Rainbow' Elvira was there, right in front of her in the orchestra pit, smiling encouragingly as she picked up the tune and started again. All her friends in the Munchkin line-up were brilliant. Without saying a word they were with her all the way, both on and off stage, smiling, or occasionally giving a secret little wink, even squeezing her hand as they danced the opening song. Luke was both funny and thoughtful. He made Belle smile when he introduced himself on stage.

'I'm Scarecrow,' he said, bowing awkwardly with his stiff arms and legs. As he bent he leaned close to Belle and tickled her face with his straw head. Giggling, she bowed back, but she didn't forget her lines, the little private joke eased her nerves and relaxed her quickly into playing Dorothy.

There was one hiccup during the second half. Part of the scenery didn't drop completely down so the Wizard of Oz's palace only had two sides and no back. It would have been all right if it had stayed up but instead it hung half up and half down, just wobbling about, disconcerting everybody. It was only Luke the comedian, with his quick wit, who had the confidence to remark on it.

'Funny looking palace for a wizard,' he joked, completely unscripted. 'Still, even wizards can't get a good builder these days!'

Almost on cue the back of the palace set dropped into place and Luke hid behind the Tin Man who hid behind the Lion who dithered from head to toe with fear. The audience laughed and applauded their impromptu act, then the show carried on without a hitch.

Seeing Belle's white face Helen whispered, 'Ignore all the noise around you and take long, deep breaths.'

Standing by Belle she breathed steadily with her.

'Breathe deep, hold and exhale slowly. Phew . . .'

Belle felt her nerves subside and she slipped into her new role like she was born for it! At the end of the performance, as the final curtain came down to tumultuous applause, Belle turned and beamed at the cast, lined up on either side of her.

'Thank you, thank you,' she whispered as the curtain rose again.

To her astonishment Helen stopped the audience mid-applause and delivered a short speech.

'I'd like you to put your hands together for an extra special girl, Belle Forest, who so heroically under-studied Dorothy this afternoon at amazingly short notice.'

As the crowd cheered and clapped Belle was propelled forward to the front of the stage by Jazz, Millie and Rozzie, all smiling from ear to ear.

'Well done, Belle,' smiled Helen as she handed her a huge bouquet of red roses.

Belle looked at the beautiful flowers and burst into

tears. Fortunately Elvira struck up the encore for 'Follow the Yellow Brick Road' and the cast moved forward to sing the final song together. As Belle smiled through her tears all the cast beamed back – apart from one member. Tracie Long looked daggers at her and even in her moment of triumph Belle shuddered as if somebody had walked over her grave.

CHAPTER SIXTEEN

★

Curtain Call

The twins' chocolate cake was indeed delicious but Belle was so tense she could hardly swallow a crumb. She now realised the enormous difference between playing the main part and simply being one of many in the chorus line. As a Munchkin she had fun, giggling and joking with her best friends backstage. As Dorothy she was permanently under pressure on stage.

'I don't know how I'll do tonight's show,' Belle fretted to Jazz as she tried to relax between shows.

'Cheer up, your parents are coming,' Jazz coaxed. 'That should help.'

'Not really,' Belle answered. 'It just makes me feel even more nervous.'

'Come on, get a grip,' Jazz teased. 'You were brilliant. Of course you can do it again.' Belle didn't look at all convinced.

'With a bit of luck Daisy might turn up.'

At six o'clock, to Belle's unspeakable relief, Daisy and her mum did show up. Both of them looked upset and very flustered.

'I am so sorry,' Belle heard Mrs Belham-Thomas say to Helen as Daisy rushed straight up to her and Jazz.

'How was it?' she gasped.

'Fine,' Belle answered. 'But it's great to see you!'

'What happened?' Jazz asked.

'My dad suddenly sprung one of his surprises on us,' Daisy said with a downward turn of her mouth. 'Sunday lunch with a colleague of his in Suffolk! Mum and I nearly passed out.'

'It must be a nightmare,' said Belle, trying to imagine herself in the same situation as Daisy. 'Never knowing what your father's going to do next.'

'The worst thing is not being able to tell him the truth,' Daisy admitted.

'And I thought things were bad for me at home,' Jazz murmured. 'It's a picnic compared to your set-up, Daisy.'

'It's lousy,' she agreed. 'Even worse for Mum. She gets so tense and upset. The trouble is she can't argue with him or refuse to go. That would give the game away and if he ever found out that I was here that would be the end of my drama club days forever.'

There was no time for any more discussion. It was getting on for six thirty and there was a lot to do. With the arrival of the leading lady Belle could start to relax and have fun on the final night. She, Jazz and the twins changed into their costumes, then sat down in a row at the dressing-table and started to apply their make-up. The twins played around with theirs, Millie painted her nose green and Rozzie painted her lips blue!

'You look more like Martians than Munchkins!' giggled Belle, who laughed so much that the tears from her eyes smudged her rouge and turned her cheeks spotty!

The only person who didn't join in the fun was Tracie Long, who glowered across the dressing-room.

'Go and ask her if she'd like another wart,' teased Belle, setting the girls off into peals of helpless giggles all over again.

They all managed to calm down during the warm-up exercises then, as they heard the audience arriving, their pulses quickened with excitement.

'Isn't it the best feeling in the world?' Belle whispered to Jazz as they peeped from the wings.

When Belle saw her family, including little Ben wide-eyed with excitement, taking their places four rows from the front she felt her heart lift and flutter.

'Want my sister!' yelled Ben over the buzz of

chatter. 'Want Belle to sing to me,' he cried as he started to clap his hands.

'Trust Ben,' said Belle, smiling fondly at the little boy's delightful antics.

There was a great atmosphere that last night. Everybody had got into their part, there were no hitches, technical or otherwise. It just went with a swing! During the interval the girls dashed back to their dressing-room for a drink and Belle, who was extremely thirsty, downed two glasses of lemon squash very quickly, then realised she was desperate for the loo! Without telling anybody where she was going Belle ran into the ladies where she pulled impatiently at her costume.

'Drat,' she muttered as she heard an ominous ripping sound. Gingerly she stepped out of her costume to inspect the damage and stared in horror at the rip in back of her tunic.

'Oh, no!' she cried out loud.

'What's wrong?' called a voice from outside the locked toilet.

Not instantly recognising the voice Belle wailed, 'My costume's ripped.'

'Hand it over,' came the reply. 'I'll take it to Gilly.'

'Tracie . . . ?' Belle asked cautiously. 'Is that you?'

157

'Yes,' Tracie answered cheerfully. 'Come on, be quick. We've got five minutes to curtain up.'

There was no time to argue and Belle, dressed only in her skimpy knickers, couldn't exactly go running down the corridor searching for Gilly! Very much against her better judgement Belle shoved the ripped costume under the toilet door.

'You will be quick?' she asked nervously.

There was no reply, just a loud bang of the door as Tracie left. Shivering in her knickers Belle sat on the toilet seat and hugged her discarded Munchkin tights to her chest, agonisingly aware of the passing of time. Without a watch she counted the seconds very, very slowly and after five lots of sixty she knew there was something wrong. When she heard the muffled curtain call, alerting the cast to the start of the second act Belle began to panic. Where *was* Tracie? How stupid of her to have even thought of trusting her. Even half naked she should have taken the ripped costume to Gilly herself. As all these arguments surged into her head Belle heard the door.

'Belle!' called Millie. 'Are you in there?'

'Yes!' cried Belle, throwing open the toilet door and peeping cautiously out.

'What's wrong?' asked Millie. 'Are you sick?'

'No, no!' spluttered Belle. 'My costume ripped and I gave it to Tracie to give to Gilly. She promised to bring it back but she hasn't . . .' Belle's voice trailed miserably away.

The look of complete incredulity on Millie's face spoke multitudes. Fortunately she didn't waste time on recriminations, she just dashed out and a few minutes later returned with a dressing-gown.

'Put this on, be quick!'

The two girls hunted everywhere but Tracie Long was nowhere to be found, unfortunately neither was Gilly. When Andy gave the stand by call Millie had no choice but to leave Belle backstage, still searching for the missing outfit.

'When you find it just slip on and join us,' she told Belle. 'Good luck.'

As the music for the second act swelled out Belle fought back bitter tears. Her parents would be out there waiting for her. Little Ben would be clapping his hands in excitement. It was the final night and she was missing it. Fighting for control she systematically searched every centimetre of the dressing-room. She was so desperate she even looked in the boys' dressing-room. The costume was nowhere to be found. In a fury she emptied out the contents of

Tracie Long's bag, it wasn't in there, neither was it in the wardrobe or the showers. The tunic had completely disappeared! As the minutes ticked away Belle knew the second act was coming to an end.

'I'm going to miss it,' she said out loud and unable to control herself a minute longer she burst into floods of hysterical tears. Gilly found her in the dressing room crying her eyes out.

'Belle! Why aren't you on stage?' she gasped.

'Tracie Long took my costume and I can't find it anywhere,' sobbed Belle wretchedly.

'I don't believe even she could sink so low,' seethed Gilly. 'Are you absolutely sure?'

'Yes. I ripped it in the toilets and she said she'd bring it to you,' Belle explained. 'I was stupid enough to believe her,' she wailed.

'Shush,' soothed Gilly, patting Belle's shuddering shoulders. 'I'll have a look now.'

'There's no point,' Belle wept. 'It's too late. They're coming to the end of the show.'

She was right. Elvira was playing the cast into the final song. Pulling the dressing-gown round her shoulders, Belle sneaked into the wings and peeped round the stage curtain. Her family were sitting in the fourth row looking very confused and extremely disappointed. Ben was sobbing and even above the tumultuous applause Belle could hear him yelling, 'Want Belle! Want Belle!'

Suddenly her eyes lit on the family she'd least expected to see in the theatre – the Khans! They were sitting just behind her family, clapping enthusiastically and smiling proudly. Belle's eyes flashed to Jazz who was on stage looking radiant with joy. The applause grew louder and the cast were showered with bouquets. Helen led them in not just one encore but two, then finally the curtain came down on an ecstatic audience. As the cast came offstage Belle waited in the wings. As each person passed they all asked the same thing, 'What happened?'

Belle didn't answer but waited, her eyes blazing with fury. When Tracie Long eventually appeared she caught hold of her arm.

'Where's my costume?' she seethed.

Tracie Long shrugged carelessly.

'I've no idea what you're talking about,' she said in a voice loud enough for everybody to hear.

'How could you do such a cruel thing?' Belle demanded, still clutching her arm.

Tracie Long shook her off and walked away but as she did so she whispered something so quietly even

Belle had difficulty hearing it. 'You were getting too big for your boots, new girl. You needed bringing down to size.'

So angry she could hardly breathe, Belle ran into the dressing-room where she threw on her clothes and dragged a damp tissue over her stage make-up.

'Stay, *please*,' begged the twins as she headed for the door.

'No!' called Belle but Jazz caught her up.

'Come on, the end of show party will cheer you up,' Jazz urged.

Belle shook her head. 'Nothing could cheer me up right now,' she whispered.

Outside in the corridor Daisy ran up. 'BELLE!' she yelled, stopping the girl in her tracks. 'Please take these,' she said, handing her a huge bouquet of white roses. 'Mum got them for you. To give you on stage,' she added, her lovely eyes filling up with tears. 'I'm so sorry,' she said as she threw her arms round Belle and hugged her.

Belle hugged Daisy tight then fled. Holding her bouquet, her face blotchy and tear-stained, Belle stepped into the foyer where her family were waiting for her.

'Belle!' cried Ben. Running forwards he threw

himself into her arms and thrust a bunch of crushed
anemones into her face. Through a mist of tears Belle
looked at the crumpled flowers and her brother's
smiling face.

'Thank you, Ben,' she whispered. 'You're the best
thing that's happened to me tonight!'

CHAPTER SEVENTEEN

★

Encore!

The flu that Belle had managed to avoid for weeks threatened to engulf her just as the wretched end of term exams started.

'I feel awful,' she croaked to Jazz after the first ghastly maths test. 'I can't tell whether it's my throat, my head or my brain.'

'Everything,' Jazz assured her.

Belle had discovered from Jazz in the playground first thing on Monday morning that there'd been an awful rumpus after she'd left the theatre on Saturday night. In the middle of the party Helen had been seen in deep conversation with Gilly who was very hot and bothered.

'A few minutes later,' Jazz told her, 'Helen walked over to Tracie Long and asked her point-blank where your Munchkin costume was.'

'Really?' gasped Belle.

'Really,' Jazz told her with relish. 'Of course face-ache Tracie lied through her teeth and pretended she hadn't a clue what Helen was talking about but Helen wasn't having any of it. She said, "If you don't deliver

164

up that costume I, and the rest of the cast, will turn this theatre upside down until we find it!" Can you imagine?' Jazz said, wide-eyed with awe. 'It was only then, with all of us eyeballing her, that Tracie cracked.' Jazz paused dramatically.

'Oh, I wish I'd been there! Go on!' Belle begged.

'She reached behind a filthy radiator and pulled out your tunic which she'd ripped into shreds.'

'No!' cried Belle, breathless. 'Then what?'

'She flung it at Helen's feet and stormed out,' Jazz said. 'And do you know what?' she added, starting to giggle. 'She still had that stupid big wart on the end of her nose!'

It was only at the lunch-time break that Belle got the chance to ask Jazz about her parents.

'Didn't you get the shock of your life when you saw them out there in the auditorium?' she said.

'I nearly died!' Jazz assured her. 'I didn't see them at all in the first half. Jamal told me they insisted on standing at the back so as not to put me off. When the second act started I was so worried about you I didn't even notice them. When I saw them I missed my timing and nearly danced off the edge of the stage!'

Belle burst out laughing. 'What did they say?'

'They loved it!' Jazz said triumphantly. 'Just loved it.'

'They weren't cross?'

'They gave me a bit of earache afterwards about not telling them the whole truth,' Jazz admitted.

'They didn't mind you appearing on stage?' Belle asked, intrigued by their change of attitude.

'No. But I think they would mind if they didn't like and trust Helen so much. They also got on really well with lots of the parents that night which made a big difference,' Jazz added.

'Wow! No more worries,' Belle said with a sigh of relief.

'Not for the moment,' said Jazz, holding up crossed fingers on both hands. 'By the way, Helen's asked us all to go and help her tidy up backstage on Wednesday night, just for an hour. Can you come?'

'I'll try,' said Belle. 'But after Saturday night's fiasco my parents aren't one bit keen on me going to the drama club again!'

*   *   *

Belle was right. Her parents weren't at all pleased.

'Why, for goodness' sake,' cried her mother. 'You virtually lived at that blooming theatre all last week!'

'I know,' Belle agreed. 'It's just to help Helen do

some tidying up backstage. She won't keep us long, I'm sure.'

'Hasn't she got a secretary who can help?' her mother snapped irritably.

'Mum . . . directors don't have secretaries,' Belle laughed. 'She had Andy, the stage-manager —'

'He could help her, surely,' Mrs Forest interrupted.

'He's gone back to college,' Belle explained. 'He's got exams next term —' she stopped dead and could have kicked herself for mentioning the dreaded word 'exams'.

'That reminds me, how did your exams go today?' asked Mrs Forest.

Belle shrugged. 'OK,' she lied. English and Geography had been the exams from hell! Belle already knew she'd done really badly in both. Still, school had broken up that afternoon and as far as she was concerned the exams could go hang until term started again in the New Year. Suddenly Ben came charging into the kitchen on his hobby-horse and nearly knocked them both flying.

'Come on, young cowboy,' said Mrs Forest firmly. 'Time for your bath.'

'Belle bath Ben,' pleaded the little boy.

'No, I'm going to drama club,' Belle told him.

'To sing?' he asked solemnly.

'No, to tidy up *The Wizard of Oz* play,' she explained.

'Don't like the Wicked Witch,' said Ben, his soft little face crumpled with fear. 'She was horrible!'

'Yes, Ben, the Wicked Witch was horrible . . .' Belle agreed. 'Probably still is,' she added under her breath.

The theatre was cold and empty after the glorious warmth and bright colour of the previous week's show. The stage was completely clear. The set had been struck, as Helen called it, which meant that everything had been removed and stored away straight after the performance. At the end of the show the props and costumes had been chucked higgledy-piggledy into big baskets backstage and this was where Helen now needed their help.

'If you see anything that's ripped or broken please leave it in the basket by the stage door for repair,' she said. 'Gilly will be going around checking everything too, but you know the old saying, many hands make light work?'

'Why is she being so thorough?' Daisy said as she, Jazz and Belle set to work. 'Usually we just chuck the stuff in the baskets and store them away.'

'Maybe they're thinking of running *Oz* again,' Jazz teased.

'Count me out,' said Daisy. 'We're off on our skiing holiday straight after Christmas.'

'That should be fun,' said Belle enviously.

Daisy turned down the corners of her pert, pink mouth.

'Not with my dad,' she answered. 'He'll be expecting me to do all the big slopes and prove how good I am. Still, the snow's pretty and Swiss chocolate is the best in the world. I'll bring you some back, I promise,' she said with a smile.

As Belle tidied away props she glanced anxiously about for Tracie Long.

'Hasn't she turned up?' she asked Luke.

'No way!' he laughed. 'Can you imagine a drama queen like her coming here just to tidy up?'

'No, I can't,' Belle answered. 'I'd be happy if she never showed up here again.'

'She will though,' Luke assured her. 'Just as soon as the next show looms she'll be back, looking for the star part.'

They worked solidly for an hour then Helen called them together.

'I've a few things to say before you go. They won't

take long,' she added with a twinkle in her eye. 'I know after last week your parents won't want any more late nights.'

'That's a relief,' muttered Jazz under her breath. 'Mine would go mad if I was late again.'

'First of all, thank you for a marvellous show and all the hard work you put in on it. Well done.'

The group beamed. This was praise indeed from Helen Powers.

'Second, have you seen the excellent reviews we got over the weekend?' As she spoke Helen handed around newspaper clippings from several local papers. 'Best Yet!' they read. 'Cambridge Super Drama Club!' and 'Brilliant Production.'

'Did any of you know,' continued Helen, with a ring in her voice that compelled attention, 'that Alan Grey, the city's Recreational and Amenities Officer, was sitting in the audience on the final night?'

They all shrugged and looked nonplussed.

'I wouldn't know him if I saw him,' Luke joked.

'Well, it just may interest you to know that he thought the production was wonderful, one of the best children's productions he's ever seen. Let me read from his letter,' Helen said as she scanned down an official letter on embossed paper. ' "If you think

your company could sustain another week's work," '
she quoted, ' "I'd like to invite them to stage *The
Wizard of Oz* at the Little Theatre on Newmarket Road.
The venue has been reserved for some time but the
touring company I had originally hoped to book has
folded. If you could discuss the matter with the Drama
Club and let me know your decision, as soon as
possible, I'd be most grateful, etc . . . etc . . ." ' Helen
finished, as she folded the letter and paused. 'Well,
what do you think?' she asked, her eyes blazing with
pride. 'It's up to you.'

There was a moment's pause before Jerome
answered in his cool, steady voice, 'Let's do it!'

'Yeah!' everybody yelled as they all went up like
rockets.

When the hullabaloo had died down Helen
mentioned some vital changes.

'First,' she said, quickly glancing over at Daisy who
was looking very disappointed, 'our lead girl won't be
here.' She waited for Daisy to answer for herself.

'I'm going away for ten days skiing,' she said slowly.

'Can I swop places?' Luke teased.

'Willingly!' Daisy answered without a moment's
hesitation, which made everybody laugh and eased
the rather awkward atmosphere.

'So it's up to you Belle, can you do it?'

Aware of Daisy's loss being her gain Belle quickly glanced over to her friend who nodded and smiled encouragingly.

'Go for it, Belle,' she said.

'Yes!' Belle cried. 'Though I might need a minder,' she added, only half joking.

'I'll mind you!' laughed Luke.

'It's a week's run, starting on the twenty-eighth of December and going through to the third January. You'll all have to get written permission from your parents – immediately. We'll be back in rehearsals on Boxing Day, ten o'clock sharp at the Little Theatre . . .'

As Helen chatted Belle's thoughts drifted off. She was going to play Dorothy again! For a whole week she'd have the star role in the Cambridge Junior Drama Club and this time nobody could take it away from her, not even Tracie Long.

'So,' said Helen rising to her feet. 'Have a happy, happy Christmas and come back ready for a return to Oz!'

As the group left the theatre, calling 'Merry Christmas' to each other, Helen stopped Belle.

'Are you ready for this?' she whispered.

Belle nodded and smiled radiantly.

'I just can't wait!' was her instant reply.

Jazz and Belle cycled home across the frosty common, their faces pink and bright against the biting cold wind.

'What do you want for Christmas?' Jazz asked.

'Magic red shoes,' smiled Belle. 'And Helen's just given them to me – on a plate!'

Laughing, the girls carried on through the drifting snow, their happy voices echoing in the velvet darkness.

'We're off to see the wizard, the wonderful Wizard of Oz . . .'

h HODDER

Another fantastic Starstruck title from
Hodder Children's Books

STARSTRUCK

CURTAIN CALL

Diane Redmond

*Belle, Jazz, Luke and Daisy. Four friends with one
aim - stardom and a life on the stage!*

Jazz has a talent for acting, but her parents don't
care. It's backstage or nothing! But being a
wardrobe mistress isn't enough for Jazz.
Somehow, she has to get into the limelight!

STARSTRUCK

THEATRE SCHOOL

Diane Redmond

*Belle, Jazz, Luke and Daisy. Four friends with
one aim - stardom and a life on the stage!*

Luke's always loved acting. And he's good at it
too! But his bullying brothers disapprove, and
this means trouble . . .

Now that his drama club have been chosen to
perform on television, will Luke's brothers leave
him alone at last? And is this the big time they've
all been dreaming of?

ORDER FORM

0 340 66104 6	**CURTAIN CALL** *Diane Redmond*	£3.50
0340 66105 4	**THEATRE SCHOOL** *Diane Redmond*	£3.50
0 340 66106 2	**ENCORE** *Diane Redmond*	£3.50

All Hodder Children's books are available at your local bookshop or newsagent, or can be ordered direct from the publisher. Just tick the titles you want and fill in the form below. Prices and availability subject to change without notice.

Hodder Children's Books, Cash Sales Department, Bookpoint, 39 Milton Park, Abingdon, OXON, OX14 4TD, UK. If you have a credit card you may order by telephone – (01235) 831700.

Please enclose a cheque or postal order made payable to Bookpoint Ltd to the value of the cover price and allow the following for postage and packing: UK & BFPO – £1.00 for the first book, 50p for the second book, and 30p for each additional book ordered up to a maximum charge of £3.00.
OVERSEAS & EIRE – £2.00 for the first book, £1.00 for the second book, and 50p for each additional book.

Name ....

Address ....

....

....
If you would prefer to pay by credit card, please complete:
Please debit my Visa/Access/Diner's Card/American Express (delete as applicable) card no:

Signature ....

Expiry Date ....